A Questionable Death

and Other Historical Quaker Midwife Mysteries

A Questionable Death

and Other Historical Quaker Midwife Mysteries

BY EDITH MAXWELL

Introduction by Victoria Thompson

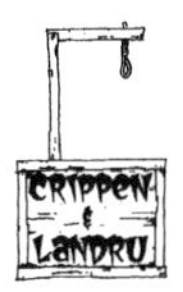

Crippen & Landru Publishers
Cincinnati, Ohio
2023

For information contact:
Crippen & Landru, Publishers
P. O. Box 532057
Cincinnati, OH 45253 USA

Web: www.crippenlandru.com
E-mail: Orders@crippenlandru.com

ISBN (softcover): 978-1-936363-74-2
ISBN (clothbound): 978-1-936363-75-9

First Edition: April 2023
10 9 8 7 6 5 4 3 2 1

For independent midwives

Janet Leigh, Peggy Thurston, and Miriam Khalsa,

who gently helped me birth my sons long ago

and showed me what a midwife-assisted birth could be,

now and in the past.

CONTENTS

Introduction
By Victoria Thompson

I'm always surprised when people tell me they don't read historical fiction. This is probably because they didn't enjoy studying history in school, and they didn't enjoy it because of the way it is taught. Nobody likes memorizing dates, but everyone enjoys gossip. Studying history should be finding out all the secrets of the past, who did what and why, and not memorizing verses like, "In 1492, Columbus sailed the ocean blue." Or maybe it was, "In 1493, Columbus sailed the deep blue sea." I can never remember.

Historical fiction is the gossip of history. L.P. Hartley said, "The past is a foreign country. They do things differently there." By reading historical fiction, we learn how people acted and did things and why thing are the way they are today. For example: Why is it called a flashlight? Because early versions only stayed on for a few seconds and then went out. They "flashed." Now, don't you feel clever for knowing that? Historical fiction makes us feel clever.

Historical fiction also is the perfect medium for examining social issues in a unique way. When we do, we learn that the more things change, the more they stay the same. In Edith Maxwell's Quaker Mystery Series, women are still more than 30 years away from winning the vote, and yet the struggles that Rose, her friends, family, and patients face are things women still struggle with today. We can see the progress we have made—or not made—and it allows us to see these issues in a whole new way. This is what Edith Maxwell does in her historicals.

As the author of a historical mystery series featuring a midwife, I have followed Edith Maxwell's Quaker Midwife Mysteries with great interest. Her books are always full of interesting period detail in addition to baffling mysteries. Readers love learning new things while being entertained by a good story, and Edith skillfully fills both needs. Midwife Rose delivers babies while living her simple life as a Quaker and solving murders into the bargain. Rose even has a bit of romance, although her beau isn't quite suitable. Things look dim for the couple, but readers will be pulling for them.

Edith's books are a feast, and in this volume, she gives us shorter entries offering the same delights. The collection begins with a never-before-published story, *In Pursuit of Justice*, that is a prequel to the series, explaining how Rose first discovered her talent for investigation.

Rose encounters *An Ominous Silence* when the train she is traveling in gets stopped by a blizzard. The details of late 19th Century train travel fascinate the reader while Rose plays Hercule Poirot on *The Orient Express,* searching for the killer among the passengers.

The Tragic Death of Mrs. Edna Fogg has Rose considering all the ways in which women are struggling against the constraints of society and how it is affecting them. She learns, to her disappointment, that doing so can also be dangerous.

The famous poet, John Greenleaf Whittier, was a real-life resident of Amesbury, where Edith's stories usually take place, and Edith brings him to life in her series, where he often appears to offer Rose counsel or to request her assistance. When there's a *Murder in the Summer Kitchen* at Whittier's home, Rose is shocked to discover who the intended victim was and races to stop another murder.

The Mayor and the Midwife work together to solve a murder with possible ties to the corrupt underbelly of New Orleans, while *The Case of the Missing Bicycle* has Rose pursuing an unlikely criminal. When Rose discovers that a woman's demise is *A Questionable Death*, she uncovers a surprising plot.

Edith even gives us a chance to get to know some of the other characters from her novels by featuring them in the role of sleuth in two of the stories. Postmistress and Rose's dear friend, Bertie Winslow, is playing matchmaker for two young people, *Adam and*

Eva, but with unfortunate consequences. *A Fire in Carriagetown* prompts Rose's niece Faith to use her own investigative skills.

Finally, Edith gives readers what they always want: a glimpse into her heroine's future. *The Management of Secrets* shows Rose a decade later when she is a wife and a mother but still has not lost her detecting skills.

Thank you, Edith, for giving us this glimpse into 19th Century New England with all its wonders and social issues. You entertain and educate us in the most delightful way.

Victoria Thompson
February 2023

In Pursuit of Justice

Author Note: This new story shows Rose Carroll in her first murder investigation. I loved digging into her backstory and depicting her while she was still a midwifery apprentice.

I stared at the note from John Greenleaf Whittier.

> *20 Twelfth Month 1886*
>
> *My dear Rose,*
>
> *Over the past year that thee has been worshipping with Amesbury Friends, I have taken note of thy particular abilities to listen, perceive, and discern. Kevin Donovan, the police detective in our fair town of Amesbury, has requested my assistance in yesterday's violent death of Friend Zachariah Woolman. In turn, I request thy presence when I meet with the detective this afternoon at three o'clock at my residence. I thought, in pursuit of justice, that thee might help tease out the facts of the homicide, such that we help the good officer to solve it.*
>
> *I am truly thy friend,*
>
> *John*

I'd heard of a murder in town, but no one had mentioned that the victim had been a member of the Religious Society of Friends.

But how could I, a midwifery apprentice, possibly help the famous Quaker poet and abolitionist, not to mention the police force? I was but twenty-four, not married nor a pillar of society, instead pursuing my dream of helping women safely birth their babies.

Still, I couldn't refuse. John Greenleaf Whittier was famed throughout the country, but we worshipped together here in Amesbury, Massachusetts. He was kindly and inquisitive, although elderly, and had taken an interest in me. The morning was young, and I had no other obligations this afternoon.

"Wait one moment, please," I said to the boy who'd delivered the short missive. I returned with a hastily scribbled reply and a coin and pressed them into his hand. "Deliver this back to John Whittier, if thee would, with my thanks."

The lad ran off. I closed my eyes and held Zachariah's released soul in the Light of God, that he might go easily. My eyes flew open as I remembered I'd attended the labor of a Lucy Woolman with my teacher and mentor, Orpha Perkins, last spring. Lucy was about ten years older than I, and she'd easily birthed her fourth, a baby girl. I'd met her husband—Zachariah—only briefly after the healthy infant and her mother were clean and presentable. Now Lucy was a widow and responsible for four little ones. My heart broke for her.

During labor, women risk death to bring forth life. On certain sad occasions, babies don't survive the ordeal, and sometimes mothers die. Not a one expects to lose the baby's father to a premature death. Who would have killed Zachariah, and why?

***

Her pregnancy near its term, Emma Gauthier struggled to sit up on the bed in her father's home at eleven o'clock that morning after Orpha had finished her antenatal examination. I hurried to support Emma, and she shot me a grateful smile. It was Orpha's practice to conduct a visit at the prospective mother's abode shortly before her due date to assure all was in order for the birth, which would, of course, take place at home.

"It's a good thing I'm not supposed to be going out." Emma gave a swipe to her wavy, honey-colored hair and a rueful glance at her swollen ankles. "I can't stuff my feet into my shoes."

"You have gained a goodly amount of weight." Orpha, a seasoned midwife, gave me a quick look. "The swollen ankles and feet are a sign you're retaining fluid. Make sure you take time to recline and elevate them above the level of your heart every day."

"That won't be so easy. Father expects me to be doing everything I did before I married and moved with Antoine to Quebec a year ago. I told him I can't." Emma let out a noisy breath. "When my husband offered to prepare meals, Father scoffed and said that was women's work. You must know, my darling husband loves me very much and would do anything for me. But Father was having none of it."

"What is thy husband's occupation?" I asked.

"He's a lawyer from a fine family in Quebec City, up in French Canada, but he likes to tinker in his spare time, invent this and that."

"I know your mother is deceased," Orpha said softly.

"Yes." Emma's pretty face fell. "She died after giving birth to my youngest sister four years ago. Mrs. Perkins, I confess to being worried. What if I die in childbirth, too?"

"Do you know why your mother perished?" Orpha asked.

"I'm not sure anybody knew. Her color was high—rather like mine, I'm afraid – and she seemed nervous. Then something burst in her brain after the birth. The doctor we summoned couldn't save her."

"That must have been so hard for thee and the whole family." I suspected it had been particularly painful for Emma and her father. "Does thee have an auntie or other older relative who might assist in thy travails?"

"Sadly, no. But my next-youngest sister, the eldest of the four who came after I was born, would like to help in any way she can." Emma raised her voice. "Jennie?"

An angular girl who looked about sixteen hurried in, tucking a lock of red hair behind her ear. A strip of cloth was wound around her palm.

"Mrs. Perkins, Rose, this is my sister Eugenia, but we call her Jennie. Sis, this is the midwife and her apprentice. They'll be here when the baby starts to come. You'll help them, won't you?"

"I guess I'll have to. Just like all the other work you left me with." Jennie turned on her heel and walked out.

"I apologize," Emma murmured. "She can be prickly. But she'll assist in any way you need her to."

"Very well," Orpha said. "Now, Mrs. Gauthier, I must insist you spend as much time as possible lying on your left side. In addition, drink plenty of water and avoid salt in the coming weeks."

"Yes, ma'am."

Orpha and I were readying our wraps when a man blustered into the room. Closer to sixty than fifty, I thought, his dark hair was streaked with white, and his spectacles repaired with wire.

"Where's that Frenchie of yours, Emmie?" he demanded.

"Antoine went out. Mrs. Perkins and Miss Carroll, this is my father, Hiram Newcastle. Father, they'll be the midwives for my birth."

"Pleased, I'm sure." His glower did not make him look pleased. "I can't find my ring, Emmie. I'm sure that no-good husband of yours took it. He's probably off pawning it right this minute."

"Your Dartmouth class ring?" Emma asked.

"Of course." He held out his right hand, palm down. The

fingers were bare. "You let me know when he returns. I'll give that Canuk what for like he's never seen."

"Antoine would never steal from you, Father." Emma stood, her color even higher than it had been before. "I fail to understand what you have against him. He's kind, he's intelligent, he's a good provider, and he loves me." She looked as if she had more to say, but she shut her mouth instead.

"We'll just be going," Orpha said softly. "Good day, sir. Mrs. Gauthier, be sure to contact me if regular pains commence before next week's visit."

***

A few minutes later, my mentor and I trudged homeward along Market Street.

"Emma's father is an unpleasant man, isn't he?" I asked.

"Mr. Newcastle isn't a happy person, certainly." Orpha took my arm.

"True, he suffered the loss of his wife. Does thee know his occupation?"

"I don't." Her gait faltered at a rough spot in the paving stones. "You know, I'm not sure how much longer I can keep working, my dear Rose. I've lived eighty years now and have lost count of how many labors I've attended."

"Thy experience is part of why thee is such a good teacher and midwife." I made sure she didn't slip as we walked, even as I hoped she wouldn't retire from the work for good long time. "Remind me why Emma's ankles would be so swollen."

"It's likely from the weight gain and not staying off her feet. She also seems to have a condition where the blood quickens. It can be dangerous."

"Does thee mean the pulse?"

"Not precisely. But it can include a nervousness, and high color in the face – higher than normal in pregnancy, I mean – and can present a threat to the mother's life."

"That sounds like the problem that her own mother had, one that led to apoplexy," I mused.

"Indeed. Thus my encouragement about the water and the salt, in particular."

Where else would I learn such valuable practices? I was grateful beyond measure Orpha had agreed to take me on as her apprentice. Six years ago, I'd helped my older sister Harriet give birth to her youngest of five, my niece Betsy, with Orpha as her midwife. It was then I knew doing that work would be my life's vocation. I'd waited several years while finishing my schooling. And I'd prayed and waited for discernment that it was the right course for me to take.

When I'd finally approached Orpha, she'd taken both my hands in hers and gazed into my eyes. "You have both the gift and the will. I shall teach you all I know."

***

John steepled his fingers and regarded the detective as we three sat in the parlor of the poet's home on Friend Street. He'd introduced me to Kevin after I arrived promptly at three o'clock. The detective was a round-headed Irishman with a flush to his cheeks and a sturdy build.

"Please lay out the facts of this tragic case, Kevin," John began, "so we may discern the way forward."

Kevin didn't seem taken aback by John's use of his Christian name, after the manner of Friends. Perhaps John had explained our faith's strong belief in equality at a prior meeting.

"Very well." Kevin bobbed his head. "Mr. Zachariah Woolman, a family man of forty, was found dead in his workshop on West Winkley Street last evening."

"How did he die?" I asked.

"My answer is not for the faint of heart, Miss Carroll. Shall I proceed?"

"I am not faint of heart, nor do I have a weak stomach.

Please go on."

"She's a midwife's apprentice," John murmured.

"Very well. The man is a tinkerer, an inventor. He had all manner of scraps of metal and wood lying about his workshop." The detective cleared his throat. "A sharp sliver of metal to the throat was the method of death."

I swallowed. "And who discovered his body?"

"His poor wife," Kevin said. "He'd gone out to the workshop behind the house after supper while Mrs. Woolman was busy with the passel of little ones. By the time she went to check on him, he was stone cold."

It was dark by a quarter past four at this time of year, and temperatures had been frigid. In the absence of snow, young and old alike had been ice skating on Clark's and Patton's ponds, as well as on Lake Gardner. Zachariah would have gone cold quickly after death unless his workshop was well heated.

John closed his eyes. Kevin gave him a quizzical glance. I suspected John was praying for Zachariah's soul. He opened them again after a moment.

Kevin went on. "I thought it might have been a common robbery gone bad, but nothing was missing except a few papers, according to the man's wife."

"I suppose she didn't see the intruder," I said.

"No, more's the pity. I have a man out in the neighborhood asking if anyone spied the scoundrel, and you can be sure I'll be talking to the victim's employer, too."

"Where did he work?" I asked.

"At the Briggs Carriage Company. Being an inventor by avocation, he worked with another innovative man at the company to create improved parts for the carriages. Springs, hinges, axles, all whatnot. I don't know the first thing about building a carriage. I do recognize a comfortable ride when I'm in one."

"Don't we all?" John stroked his snowy chinstrap beard. "Particularly those of us in the winter of our lives."

"Now, then, I don't want to be taking up your whole afternoon." Kevin stood. "What I ask of you Quakers, should you be willing, is to find out what you can among the members of your church. I don't mean to imply in any way, let me assure you, that one of yours murdered the fellow. But someone might have heard a bit of gossip, a snatch of conversation, a piece of information that could shed light on who in tarnation might want to kill a peace-loving family man like Woolman."

"Very well, Kevin," John said.

The detective gave his head a shake. "I don't know what this world is coming to, when a gentleman is brutally killed only days before our blessed Lord's birth." The Irishman crossed himself and clapped his hat on his head. "Good day to yeh, now."

***

After I left John's, I thought a visit to new widow Lucy Woolman would be in order. The poor woman had to be reeling from the shock. I hoped her mother, or someone, was with her providing support, both emotional and practical.

A few minutes later, an older lady with Lucy's baby on her hip opened the door of the Woolman home on West Winkley Street.

"Good afternoon, ma'am. I'm Rose Carroll, midwife, and I assisted with the birth of this sweet child. I've just heard of Zachariah's passing and wondered if I might pay Lucy a visit."

"Of course, except she's asleep, finally. I'm Eliza, Lucy's mother." She made a *tsk*ing noise. "Who would want to kill poor Zachariah? He was a gentle soul in this cruel world of ours. Please come in, if thee'd like."

"If thee doesn't mind, could I possibly take a look at his workshop?"

"But that's where the wretch, whoever he was, ended my son-in-law's life."

"I know."

She peered at me. "Is thee a detective? One of those Pinkerton girls?"

"Not at all. I'm a midwife's apprentice. But the local police detective has asked John Whittier and me to assist him." Kevin hadn't exactly requested that we do actual police work. Still, I felt drawn to uncovering the facts and seeking justice for Lucy's beloved husband.

"Very well. It's around the back. Do return at a later time and see my daughter. I'm sure thee would bring her comfort."

I thanked her. I smiled at the baby and laid my hand on her soft, innocent cheek, then made my way to the workshop.

It was as Kevin had described: a tinkerer's workplace. The weak afternoon light from a west-facing window lit the room, but the illumination wouldn't last long.

I stood without touching anything, taking it in. In a corner lay a small heap of wood shavings and odd bits of metal, the latter with angry-looking sharp edges. Next to a workbench, a stool had been toppled. A dark patch on the floor was likely Zachariah's blood, a sight that made me shiver. On the bench next to a rough model of a wheeled conveyance lay drawings. A rack on the wall above the table was filled with neatly hung woodworking tools, metal snips, screwdrivers, saws, and other work implements.

With so many sharp tools, why had the killer chosen a scrap from the floor? He must have worn heavy gloves so as not to cut his hand. I girded myself, trying to picture what had happened. Kevin had said the only things missing were some papers. From that pile of drawings? Perhaps they'd been plans for an invention. Zachariah could have surprised the murderer when he came out here after supper.

If they'd known each other, would they have argued? What had moved the killer to take Zachariah's life? I'd heard, over the years, more than one person in a fit of anger say, "I'd like to kill him." My own brother-in-law was given to moods and had uttered those words. But he would never cross that line and actually do the deed.

The sunlight glinted off a small object on the rough wood floor. I stepped nearer with care not to disturb anything and squatted to examine it. My eyes widened at the sight of a gold signet ring. I drew out my handkerchief and picked it up. The words engraved on the flattened top read, DARTMOUTH COLLEGE.

This might be Emma's father's ring. If so, he could be Zachariah's murderer. But why?

***

After pondering what I should do, I approached the police station the next morning, the Dartmouth ring carefully secured in my handkerchief inside a small reticule. Before I could mount the granite steps, the door opened and Hiram Newcastle strode out onto the landing, pulling on his gloves against the cold.

"Good morning, Hiram."

He scowled. "Do I know you?"

"I'm Rose Carroll, one of the midwives who will be attending thy daughter's birth. We met yesterday."

"Yes, yes. You'd better take good care of my girl and make sure my grandson has a safe passage."

"That is certainly our plan."

"Very well. Good day, then." He touched his bowler and hurried away.

Of course, we had no way of knowing whether Emma would produce a boy or a girl. This man had fathered five daughters. He probably longed for a grandson.

Several moments later I sat across from Kevin in his cramped office, a battered desk between us.

"Do you already have a few tidbits for me, Miss Carroll?" he asked

"Please call me Rose," I said.

"Oh, no, I couldn't possibly. What would me sainted mother

say?"

"I would prefer it."

"It'll be Miss Rose, then. That'll have to do."

I smiled. "Very well. I think I might have found something useful. It, in fact, relates to a man I just saw leaving the station."

"Hiram Newcastle?" Kevin's voice rose.

"Yes. You see, my teacher and I are the midwives for his eldest daughter, who is due to give birth within the next few weeks. I was there yesterday morning, and he accused her husband, Antoine Gauthier, of stealing his Dartmouth College ring."

"Did he, then?"

"Yes. After our meeting at John's yesterday, I went to pay a visit to Lucy Woolman. I helped deliver her baby last spring. She was asleep, though, so I asked her mother if I could view Zachariah's workshop."

Kevin blinked. "We did search the place, you realize."

"As is rightly thy job to do, but I wanted to see for myself. I appear to have found an item thee and thy officers missed." I drew out the ring and unwrapped it. "It seems Mr. Newcastle might have paid Zachariah a visit."

"Well, I'll be gobswoggled." He took the proffered ring and held it up to the light, turning it this way and that, squinting at the inside. "Looks like it might have something etched in there. I'll take it to my jeweler friend for an inspection."

"I also spied papers with drawings on them. Are they plans for inventions?"

"You do have a keen eye, Miss Ca—Miss Rose. Plans, they are. The Woolman missus said her husband had been working hard on some new contraption he hoped to sell to Mr. Briggs. She said those particular drawings are missing." He ran a hand over his round head. "Funny thing. Our Mr. Newcastle came in this morning to insist his French-Canadian son-in-law stole the plans, that he wants to take them back to Canada and sell them there."

"Did he have any evidence to back up his claim?"

"Not one speck," Kevin replied. "And no plausible reason, either."

"I wonder how Hiram even knew about the plans."

"I asked him that selfsame question. He claims he's also a tinkerer and had spoken with the victim about the invention last week." He tapped his temple. "Believe you me, Miss Rose, I'll be calling him back for another little chat before too long."

***

I perched next to Lucy Woolman on her settee. She held her sleeping baby. A corner of the sitting room was devoted to tin toys and wooden blocks, with a rag doll sitting astride a stuffed horse.

Investigating aside, I still wanted to see how Lucy was faring. I'd made my way here after leaving the police station.

"Thank thee for coming, Rose." Her face was tear-stained and drawn, her eyes haunted. "I don't know how I shall go on. Four mouths to feed and no husband. I miss him so, and I only want to be in heaven with him."

"I know. I also know thy children need thee, Lucy."

She gazed at her baby's face, smoothing the infant's fine hair. "And they shall have me. But my heart is truly broken."

"Zachariah wasn't a frequent attender at Friends worship, was he?"

"No." Her smile was wan but fond. "He preferred to do his tinkering when the children and I were out on a First Day morning. He said he could visit with God on his own. I didn't try to stop him."

Thus the reason I wasn't acquainted with Zachariah beyond the birth last spring. "Lucy, stop me if this is too painful, but I wondered if thee saw anything that night. Did anyone come by to see thy husband?"

"The police asked me the same question, but at the time I was too distraught to think clearly. I know I was busy with the little ones after supper. Once the others were asleep, I sat at the window nursing this sweet child." She gazed into the distance as if thinking. "I'm rather certain I saw a person round the corner of the house to the back.

My pulse increased. "What could thee see about this person? Tall or short? Slender or robust? Any facial features at all?"

"I'm sorry, Rose. It was dark, I was distracted, and I caught only a glimpse. I can say he seemed tall and had a narrow profile."

"Thee knows it was a man."

"Actually, I don't. The person wore a long coat. It could have been covering skirts, I suppose."

Or a tall woman disguising herself in a man's trousers. But who?

***

I relaxed knitting after supper at six-thirty that evening in the ladies' boardinghouse where I resided. Orpha and I hadn't had any antenatal appointments during the day, and I'd spent the afternoon perusing Leishman's *A Study of Midwifery* for details about Emma's quickened blood, color, and nervousness, not to mention the swollen ankles.

When a knock now came at the front door, one of other boarders fetched me.

"Yes?" I asked at the door. I caught my breath at a biting wind blowing in. The temperature had dropped sharply since I'd returned home at midday.

Once again, a lad pushed a note at me. I read the message from Orpha and my heart sank.

> *Received word from Emma Gauthier that her labor has begun in earnest. I am poorly this evening. Please attend her and I'll be along as I'm able. She's only two weeks before her due date,*

so the baby should be mature enough to thrive.

Don't worry, Rose. You are well capable to handle any complications that might arise. Have faith in yourself.

I dug a coin out of my pocket and handed it to the boy. I supposed there was nothing for it but to pack up my birthing satchel, don my wraps, and head out into the cold.

Despite Orpha's confidence in me, I was worried. I'd never handled a birth entirely on my own. First babies could come quickly, but more often took their time prompting their mother's body to open sufficiently for the birth. Well, I would do what needed to be done.

I paused before knocking at the house. Despite the frigid breeze, I closed my eyes to hold Emma and her infant in God's Light. And myself, as well, that I might be able to guide them both to safety.

The door opened. Hiram Newcastle barreled out, nearly knocking me over. He stopped and stared.

"You the midwife?"

"Yes."

"Well, get in there! What in blazes are you waiting for?" He rushed off, to where I couldn't guess.

***

Emma was doing reasonably well so far. It was her husband who wasn't faring well, hovering like a helpless hen. She finally convinced poor Antoine to take himself off to her uncle's home for the evening. Perhaps that was where her father had disappeared to, as well.

Emma and I were able to converse a bit between contractions. She asked how I found my way to my calling, and I explained about attending Betsy's birth. At one point I asked what Hiram did for a living.

"He fancies himself an inventor. Jennie likes to tinker with him. After Mother died, he left a perfectly good position as an accountant. He'd hoped to sell his invention to one of the carriage companies, but no one wanted it. So now he's a lowly clerk, and he's not a bit happy about it."

"Was he friendly with a man named Zachariah Woolman? He was also a tinkerer."

"I think he mentioned him once." She let out a moan and went into herself during the contraction.

Maybe her father murdered Zachariah to steal his plans, dropping his ring in the process. I immediately scolded myself for thinking about homicide during the labor of a woman under my care. I glanced at the open door to see a shadow on the hallway wall.

Emma's sister Jennie popped her head in at nine o'clock to say she was going to bed. She didn't offer any help.

"Wait," I said. "I will need two basins, one filled with clean water, plus a pitcher of clean water and a stack of clean cloths, please, before thee retires."

Jennie pulled a face but did as I asked.

Emma's face contorted. "Here comes another one."

Jennie began backing away, a horrified look on her face. "Is that all, Miss Carroll?"

"Yes, thank thee."

By ten o'clock, Emma's pains were more intense but not exceedingly close together. I counseled her to change positions, and I wiped her brow with a damp cloth. She tried to be stoical but couldn't avoid a goodly measure of both groans and cries.

Orpha never appeared. I didn't know what ailed her except that she was increasingly frail with age. But I didn't have more than a moment to worry about my mentor's wellbeing, or about murder, for that matter. Emma needed all my attention.

***

By the wee hours of the morning, the poor thing was exhausted. I encouraged her to cat-nap between contractions. I sat in a chair by her bed and snoozed when she did. With her weight gain and her swollen feet, I wasn't surprised the labor was long-lasting. First-time mothers rarely had it easy.

The pains picked up shortly before dawn. After a full hour of pushing, Emma birthed a hearty baby boy at eight forty-five. At the cry of the infant, Jennie finally made an appearance.

"Thee has a nephew," I told her.

"That's fine. You're all right, Emmie?" She stayed in the doorway.

Seeing her there brought to mind that shadow I'd noticed last evening. Had that been her listening to Emma telling me about Hiram's dashed dreams?

"I am. Can you please fetch Antoine at Uncle's and tell him he's a father?" Emma gazed at the baby in her arms.

Jennie pressed her lips together. She turned away, muttering something about "beck and call."

I finished cleaning up Emma. I tidied everything else, washed my hands, and helped her nurse the baby. I hesitated to leave until her husband or Jennie had returned, although I thought he would be more of a help than her sister. Still, I was eager to pay Kevin Donovan a visit and share a few thoughts.

Finally the new little family was happily united. Hiram never reappeared. I told Emma I'd be back the following day to check on her and asked her husband to send for me if Emma began bleeding in excess or had severe pains. I said goodbye to Jennie. She barely acknowledged me. The younger children must have been off with a neighbor, as there had been no evidence of them during my stay.

I walked out into a sunny but bitterly cold winter's day. I wanted to see how Orpha fared, but the detective came first. I'd given my word to both him and John.

***

After I delivered my thoughts to Kevin, I visited Orpha, who sat in her usual rocking chair.

"I'm feeling better now, Rose, but I was dizzy last evening," she said. "It wouldn't have been prudent for me to venture out. And I have great confidence in you. Tell me, did Mrs. Gauthier suffer any complications?"

"No. Her labor lasted more than twelve hours, but that's not so long for a first-time mother. She pushed for an hour, but she produced a healthy baby boy, and a big one. Nine pounds, twelve ounces, Orpha."

"Big babies usually survive with the most success. They have fat stores and nicely developed lungs that stand them well in case they fall ill. Did the sister we met assist you?"

"Only in the most minimal of ways. I'd have awoken her if need be, but I didn't have to." Speaking of Jennie, I wondered if Kevin was at this moment doing what I'd suggested.

Orpha tilted her head. "A penny for your thoughts?"

"Oh, it's nothing." I didn't want to burden her with my ideas about Zachariah's death. But the woman did have an uncanny ability to see into my soul.

***

I once again sat in John Whittier's parlor that afternoon. I'd been restless at home after I'd left Orpha's. The note summoning me to John's at two o'clock was most welcome. It had said only that Kevin wished to speak with both of us.

"Shall we pray while we await the good detective?" The poet folded his hands and closed his eyes.

I did likewise. I tried to hold Hiram and Jennie in the Light. Lucy and her children. Emma and Antoine and their newborn son. But my thoughts weren't peaceful, and I shifted in my chair, restless with wanting to know what Kevin would say.

At last John's housekeeper ushered in the detective, now red-cheeked from the cold.

"Well, Miss Rose, your tip was most useful," he said.

John raised a single white eyebrow.

I cleared my throat. "I told thee, Kevin, that I spoke with Lucy Woolman. She said she couldn't be sure if the tall person with the narrow profile she'd seen the night of her husband's murder was a man or a woman wearing a long coat. Last evening, as I attended Emma Gauthier in her labor, she mentioned that her sister Jennie loved tinkering with their father. He had tried to sell his invention to the carriage companies, but none would take it. Emma also thought her father had visited Zachariah."

"It was Hiram Newcastle we suspected all along," Kevin added. "Despite his claims that Antoine Gauthier was the thief and killer. And you'd found his ring in the victim's workshop."

John gazed at me. "But thee thought differently."

"As of this morning, I did. Jennie, who is sixteen, deeply resented having to do all the housework and care of the younger children after Emma married and moved to Quebec. Jennie still does. I thought perhaps she was the one who killed Zachariah and stole his plans for a new carriage invention. She was also an inventor and would have been able to see the value in the idea. I think she hoped she could sell it elsewhere and enable her father to hire a maid or a housekeeper to relieve her of her burden. The final bit was seeing her right hand with a bandage across the palm."

"As you relayed to me this morning," Kevin said. "I obtained a search warrant for the house, and we went straight away there. Sure enough, Miss Newcastle had secreted the plans under the mattress of her bed."

"Did she confess her crimes?" John asked.

"That, and then some. She sang like a canary gleeful to finally unload all the ways she felt downtrodden and burdened." Kevin shook his head in wonder. "She even called out her own father for being heartless and impractical. She's now behind bars and under the care of a police matron."

"The poor girl didn't feel loved nor cared for," I murmured. "She was hurting."

"I shall pray for the ease of her soul," John said.

Kevin made a small *harrumph* as he stood. "That's all well and good, Mr. Whittier. Right now I'm off to tell a grieving wife we've made an arrest not only in the theft of her husband's property but in the case of his homicide."

"Will Jennie receive a measure of leniency for her youth?" I asked.

"Perhaps." Kevin clapped his police hat on his head. "Good day to you both. Miss Rose, I know I asked you to keep your eyes and ears out about this case, and I'm relieved you weren't put at risk. But please do avoid further close encounters with murderers."

To my surprise, I'd found acting the sleuth satisfying, especially as I hadn't encountered danger to my person. I'd helped accomplish the pursuit of justice, despite the pain of discovering that a girl was the killer. Still, I had every intention of complying with Kevin's advice. I planned to avoid any and all homicides – and their instigators – in the future.

An Ominous Silence

Author Note: This story takes Rose and her apprentice, Annie Beaumont, out of town on a train to Montreal. I searched out a trains afficionado who advised me on late nineteenth-century rail travel.

Silence, both peaceful and ominous, jolted me awake. I lay in the upper berth in the Grand Trunk Line sleeping compartment I shared with my apprentice in midwifery, Annie Beaumont, who still slept below. Our next stop was scheduled to be at the Canadian border shortly after dawn. But it was still dark, and the car was not rumbling and clacking along the tracks, nor swaying to and fro as it had since we'd boarded in Portland, Maine, yesterday evening.

Rummaging under my pillow, I retrieved both spectacles and pocket watch. The low light from outside the privacy curtains illuminated the watch just enough to show the time: five in the morning. *What?* When I peeked behind the window shade the porter had pulled down the night before, I understood. I knew it had been risky to travel from our bustling mill town of Amesbury, Massachusetts, to Montreal in March, a time when winter still held the region in its chilly grasp. I'd been invited to a gathering of midwives, though, and I'd very much wanted Annie, originally a French-Canadian herself, to meet several famous teachers in our field.

It appeared we would arrive late. All I could see outside was white. Clumps of snow sticking to the glass. Snowflakes blowing in the wind. White bulky monsters of snow-covered pines standing sentry against a dark sky.

Perhaps an avalanche here in the White Mountains had covered the tracks. Or had an unpredicted storm blown in? Possibly both. I fought down a moment of panic. I had no idea how long it would take the railroad to clear the tracks, or if help could even reach us. What if the train exhausted its supply of food, or of coal? *No.* I shook my head. This was 1888 in New Hampshire, after all, not a century earlier nor out west on a northern prairie. Modern towns were everywhere. We wouldn't be stranded for long.

The sensible thing in this silence would be go back to sleep, but my concerns had me too wrought up to do so. Instead I pulled on my dress and shoes and climbed quietly down the cloth ladder.

"What time is it?" Annie asked in a sleepy voice.

"Five. I couldn't sleep, but thee should."

She nodded and rolled over.

My woolen shawl wrapped around my shoulders, I slipped through the heavy curtains into the aisle. If I could find a porter, I might be able to learn something about our situation.

I passed the curtain-shielded berths holding the very pregnant French-Canadian wife I'd met last evening. A grief-stricken Marie-Claire Peel had told me her father had passed away suddenly and she was traveling home from Maine to Quebec to be with family. Her maid traveled with her, as did her rather overbearing American husband, Vernon Peel, a banker in Portland who occupied the adjoining berths. I'd told Marie-Claire I was a midwife, and if she had any worries about her condition, she was welcome to solicit my assistance. Vernon, a florid, breathless man, had snorted. "She'll have a proper doctor when her time comes, not some country midwife."

I had smiled. "I'm sure she'll be well looked after." While Marie-Claire seemed to be far along in her pregnancy, we expected only a fifteen-hour train ride. I very much doubted she'd be in labor before we arrived in Montreal.

I shrugged off the memory. Curious. Not a porter in sight, nor any other passenger. I made my way down the passageway between the curtained-off berths. Yesterday I'd had to proceed with care, making sure the movement of the train didn't send me careering into the wall or a fellow traveler. Not today. A snore followed by a snort drifted out of one berth, while in another a child whimpered. The scent of warm human bodies held a back note of soot.

At last I spied a black-jacketed porter, Spencer, who stood conferring with a passenger.

"Excuse me, Spencer. Can thee tell me what has happened, please?"

The passenger studied me for a moment, almost certainly trying to figure out why I'd said "thee" instead of "you." As a Quaker, I was accustomed to such reactions.

"We're stuck in the snow, Miss Carroll," Spencer said. "We're in a cut, there's a slide just ahead, and the tracks are covered by five feet of new drift." He was a man well along in years, with a trim build, neat silver hair, and a quiet manner.

The other man, both unshaven and uncombed in contrast, nodded gravely. I'd seen him in the café parlor car after dinner, but I hadn't been introduced to him. At first he'd been carousing at the bar with Vernon Peel and then had argued with him in a belligerent tone.

"And the driver can't push through the drifts?" I asked, although the answer seemed obvious.

"No, miss. One foot, two feet, certainly. Not five."

"How shall we be rescued, then?" I tried to keep concern out of my voice.

"I could go out there and commence to shovel, if that'd help." The passenger spoke with breath reeking of stale alcohol through his grin. His high collar had sprung free of one button and rubbed against his neck.

"Now, Mr. LeMoyne, that won't be necessary," Spencer said. "When we don't arrive on time, Boston & Maine will send out train plows and meet us from the nearest maintenance station up ahead and possibly from the one behind, as well. Both of which I'm afraid are some distance away, and they can't begin until the sun comes up. We've also sent out a couple of men to make the trek to the nearest town to telegraph word of our predicament. Rescued we shall be."

"As you wish." The passenger glanced at me. "Adoniram LeMoyne, miss. At your service." He made a mock bow. "But you can call me Ade. All my friends do."

"I am Rose Carroll. I'm pleased to make your acquaintance, Ade, and hope you'll call me Rose." I watched him lurch down the corridor, weaving back and forth as if the car was still moving. I hoped he was headed for his compartment to sleep off the drink. Could he possibly have been imbibing all the night long?

I decided to continue to the café car to see if I could scare up a cup of coffee so early. I'd almost reached the passageway to the next car when I heard running footsteps. Ade came sprinting toward Spencer. I hurried back that way.

"Help!" His voice was low and urgent as he grabbed Spencer's arm. "Come quickly. He's dead!"

***

I stepped back from Vernon Peel's still form in the bottom berth. I'd checked his neck for a pulse, but his already cool skin had told me the verdict. A hand-wringing Spencer, who'd gladly accepted my offer of help, and a distraught Adoniram crowded behind me.

"Yes, I'm afraid he's dead," I murmured. But why, how? I wouldn't be surprised if heart failure caused his demise. With his red face and breathless manner, plus his girth, he'd clearly been a man to ignore his own health. Rather than a person who enjoyed long walks, fresh foods, and abstinence from intoxication, Vernon looked like a man who indulged in rich dishes, tobacco, and drink. To wit, a pewter mug from the café car lay abandoned at the end of the berth.

I turned and surveyed my companions' faces. "Was thee sharing this compartment with Vernon?" I asked Ade.

"Why, yes."

A nod from Spencer confirmed it.

"I'd just come in to take my sleep and there he was," Ade went on. "I'd met him on the platform in Portland and he invited me to ride with him, since his wife had a separate compartment with her maid. I'd decided to take this trip at the last moment but could secure only a common coach ticket, not one on the sleeping car. Vern and I are old friends, and we..." He shaded his eyes with his hand and turned away.

"I'll have to inform Mrs. Peel," Spencer murmured, his brow knitted and his eyes tensed. "And the police, when we make contact with the outside world again."

"The police, you say?" Ade whirled, suddenly over his grief. "Why on earth, man?"

"It's procedure, sir. An unattended death while in transit always demands notifying the authorities."

My mind went to work on that one. Perhaps the death hadn't been from natural causes. What if someone on the train had murdered Vernon in his sleep? Ade himself had been arguing with his so-called friend just last night. Vernon could have other acquaintances on the trip, as well. Back home, I'd been in a position to help our town's police detective solve several murders in recent years and my brain now began to sort through the possibilities. Ade's sorrow had looked genuine, but he now seemed alarmed at the prospect of police. Why?

Spencer cleared his throat. "Miss Carroll, I wondered if you might accompany me to notify Mrs. Peel. Considering her delicate condition, I'm afraid learning of her husband's demise might cause her extreme distress."

"Of course I will. She's just next door, isn't she?" With the way sound traveled through the curtains, I'd be surprised if she hadn't heard.

"Yes, miss." He closed the curtains in front of the berths.

Heads with wide eyes had popped out between other curtains in the car, but Spencer admonished them all to go back to sleep, that everything was under control.

Marie-Claire stood in front of the adjacent berths, clutching a wrapper that barely stretched around her nightgown. Her dark eyes were wide, and her petite features drawn into a mask of horror. She'd heard. She searched our faces. The stern visage of Eugenie, her maid, appeared from the upper berth above Marie-Claire, framed by the curtains.

"*Mon Dieu*, what has 'appened?" Marie-Claire's gaze fell on Ade. "Monsieur LeMoyne, who is dead?" The word "who" came out more like "oo."

"Marie-Claire, perhaps thee would like to sit down first," I ventured.

She stared at me. "Who are you, again?"

"Rose Carroll, midwife. We met in passing last evening."

She nodded. "But I must know now, who is dead?"

"I regret to inform you, ma'am, that your husband became deceased during the night," Spencer said gently.

Marie-Claire's hand tightened on her shawl until her skin was the color of bleached linen, but she didn't sway. She shook her head, fast. "It must be a mistake. Monsieur Peel cannot be dead."

"I'm afraid he is." I also spoke in a soft voice.

She nodded twice, slowly, making a *tsking* sound. "It was his heart. I told him. Now you must show me." She lifted her chin.

Eugenie murmured something to Marie-Claire in French. I'd been studying French, because I was often called to attend the births of French-Canadians in my town, but I didn't catch what she said.

"*Non*, Eugenie. I will go."

"Very well, Madame."

Spencer offered his arm, but the new widow padded past him and slid open the curtains. I watched as she knelt in front of the berth and crossed herself. She stroked Vernon's forehead, speaking privately to him. She clasped her hands and lowered her face, still murmuring. She touched her fingers to her lips and then to his before turning a wet face to gaze at Spencer.

"Now I need the help, *s'il vous plaît*." She extended her hand for Spencer to hoist her up. "Why the train is not moving? We must bring home my husband's body."

Spencer explained about our being snowed in. Eugenie shouldered past me, now fully dressed in her severe black dress, her slate-gray hair pulled back in an equally severe knot.

"Come and lie down, Madame. This is a terrible shock." She helped Marie-Claire back into her berth even as Spencer closed the curtains on the late Vernon Peel.

***

I sat with my coffee in the café car gazing at the snowy wonderland. It didn't seem so wonderful now we were stuck in it. Ade LeMoyne stood at the bar, one foot on the brass rail, a pewter tankard in front of him. Ale for breakfast, no doubt.

I considered Marie-Claire's reaction to the death. She had seemed sad but not surprised that Vernon was gone, and had not appeared as overcome with grief as some widows I'd seen.

My thoughts moved to Vernon himself. How had he died? His wife certainly thought it was from heart failure. But yards away from me stood a man who shared the compartment, who'd had a public and loud dispute with the deceased. I needed to get back to the body to check, in the absence of police, whether any clues remained as to Vernon's manner of death. We'd not even checked for a wound on his body, blood on the back of his head, or any puncture marks. I knew people were murdered in all kinds of ways beyond the obvious ones of gunshot and stabbing. Perhaps Spencer could be convinced to allow me some further investigation, despite the cordage he'd strung in front of the curtained berths and a neatly lettered sign that read, KEEP OUT. If it was a crime scene, it was hardly well secured.

In the meantime, I'd see what I could find out from Adoniram. I drained my coffee and approached the bar. "I'm very sorry about the death of thy friend, Ade." I slid onto a stool next to him.

"Thank you, miss. But tell me, why do you talk so funny,?"

I smiled. "I am a member of the Religious Society of Friends. A Quaker, if thee will. We believe in equality, and do not practice the use of titles. As for the archaic manner of speaking, that is too long a story to bore thee with this morning. In turn, tell me how thee knew Vernon?"

"We were Harvard men together, of course. Drifted apart a bit in recent years, don't you know, but when I saw him there on the platform it was like no time had passed." He shook his head in a sad gesture. "I hate the thought that the last words we exchanged were angry ones."

"I saw a bit of that exchange. What was thy dispute with him?"

He gazed at me with watery, bloodshot eyes and drained his tankard before answering. "You might have noticed he's had a bit more, ah, success than I myself have achieved. I merely asked for a small loan to tide me over until a big business venture comes through, but he was having none of it. Got quite self-righteous, going on about morality, the evils of gambling, and such. Not to speak ill of the dead, of course."

"Of course not." What he described didn't seem like the kind of argument over which to murder someone, but who knew? "Are there other acquaintances of thine here on the train? From thy Harvard days, I mean?"

"Not that I've seen. But if they haven't come into this car, I wouldn't have then, would I?" He gestured to the bartender. "Fill 'er up my man, will you?"

The door to the car burst open. Annie rushed toward me, her shawl and her red hair flying behind her. "Come quickly. Mrs. Peel is having pains!"

***

After I took a moment to wash my hands and grab the birthing kit with which I always traveled, I hurried to Marie-Claire's side. On the way from the café car I'd instructed Annie to wash up and tidy her appearance. I'd need her assistance if the pains turned out to be true labor. I didn't know if Marie-Claire had received antenatal care, or if this was her first child or her fifth. It didn't matter. If her baby and her body had chosen today for the birth, today was when it would be.

But how could we possibly help her give birth in a space essentially open to all the other passengers? I'd stopped Spencer. "Is there somewhere we can move Marie-Claire? It appears her baby is on its way and she needs privacy..."

His eyes went wide, but being the competent man he was, I saw the wheels turning in his brain.

"I might have an idea."

We were blessedly ensconced in an empty but luxurious private car several minutes later. Spencer had said the railroad was transporting it to Montreal for its new owner. Marie-Claire lay on the hastily made-up berth at the end of the car with Eugenie hovering nearby.

"I need light," I told Eugenie. "Please raise the shades and turn up the lamp." I perched on the edge of the berth even as Marie-Claire let out a cry. I quickly noted the time.

"*Ça fait mal*," she wailed. "Miss Carroll, it hurts."

"And I am here to help thee." When the pain seemed to have passed, I palpated her belly with both hands, glad to feel a fetus of a hearty size. "Good. The baby is head down and in an advantageous position. I'll listen to his heart now." I drew out my Pinard horn and pressed it against her belly, listening through the other end to a good fast heartbeat. "All is well. Tell me when thy baby was supposed to arrive."

"Not until next month. Will he survive if he comes now?"

"Not to worry. It seems of a healthy size for this stage. Let us wait and see if the pains--"

She cried out and I checked the time again. Two and a half minutes since the last one began.

I glanced up. "Does she have other children?" I asked Eugenie, who stood with hands tightly clasped. "Has thee ever assisted at a birth?"

"Oh, no, miss. This is her first. And I have no experience with such matters as childbirth." From the set of her mouth, it looked like she wasn't interested in having any, either.

I sat with Marie-Claire for the next hour as her pains grew closer together and more intense. I checked the entrance to her womb and found it well along the path to being fully open. I asked Eugenie to fetch Annie for me and told the maid she might as well go and breakfast, that we would be fully occupied here.

"Madame. Peel, *ça ne vous dérange pas*?" You don't mind?

Marie-Claire just waved the question away. "*Vas-y*." Go ahead.

After her maid left, she grabbed my arm. "I never wanted a baby," she said in a hoarse whisper. "But Monsieur. Peel, he forced himself on me, said we must have children. Now he's dead and I will have one, anyway." She wiped away a tear. "It was a terrible marriage, Rose. Eugenie, she saw my suffering." She let out a deep grunt. "Here is another."

Annie slid through the door, sleeves pushed up. "What can I do?"

I stood and spoke in a low voice. "First, please go to the café car and bring me a pot of boiled water."

"All right."

I returned to Marie-Claire's side. Had she devised a way to do away with her husband here on the train? Annie returned with the pot of water and an odd look on her face.

"Stay with her a while, please," I said. "The contractions are intensifying, but her womb is not yet fully open. I'll return in just a few minutes."

***

I reached over Vernon's body and opened the shade. I knelt in the still-ominous absence of train noises, my gaze traveling over every square inch of the berth. Luckily Spencer had not objected to my request to investigate. Telling him of my sleuthing successes persuaded him to allow my entrance. I'd ducked under the cord and closed the curtains after me.

Vernon lay fully dressed except for tie and jacket. I opened his shirt and saw no bullet holes or blood on him anywhere, nor bruises. With some difficulty I half-rolled his heavy inert body away from me, but the back of his head and neck were intact and blood-free. I let him roll back. When he did, his head followed all the way to face me, and with his eyes still open, it was not a pleasant sight. I pushed his head gently back and drew my hands over his lids. I sniffed, detecting a noxious odor in the air. Was it male sweat combined with death, or something else? A poison? I leaned in and smelled Vernon's face near his mouth and nose. That was where the scent originated.

I sat back on my heels. His body was still pliable, so his death had not been early in the evening, but I already knew that. Perhaps the bartender could tell me what time Vernon returned to his compartment.

I reached for the pewter mug and sniffed it, detecting the same unpleasant smell. If Vernon's death had not been a natural one, poison might well be the culprit. And if it hadn't been injected, this cup could be very important evidence.

Concealing the mug in my skirts, I hurried back to my compartment. It was past time for me to return to Marie-Claire, to the car now become a birthing chamber.

When I did, Annie had her hands full. She was stroking Marie-Claire's forehead, urging her not to push despite the guttural noises the mother-to-be was emitting. The look my apprentice gave me was both exasperated and grateful. I quickly mouthed, "Sorry," to Annie and washed my hands at the washbasin in the corner.

"Marie-Claire, it sounds like thee is ready to birth thy child. I'll check the opening as soon as this pain has passed." I waited until she closed her eyes and lapsed into heavy exhausted breathing before sliding my hand into her passageway. Good. A full fist's-worth. I slid my hand out and nodded to Annie as I wiped it off on a piece of linen. "Boost her up. Let us meet this baby."

Annie gently assisted Marie-Claire to assume a more upright position with bent knees.

"With the next pain, I want thee to push with all thy might." I had a fear, with her expressed unwillingness to assume the mantle of motherhood, that she might hold back the birthing process without meaning to. I'd seen it before. I took the moment of respite to close my eyes and silently hold the birthing mother and her infant in the Light of God for safe passage.

My fears blessedly did not come to pass. By the time an hour had elapsed, Marie-Claire held a small but healthy daughter. My simple birthing kit had sufficed, with Annie's help, and the birth had proceeded with no problems. The new mother gazed with surprise at the blanketed newborn girl in her arms, an infant watching her with the calm dark eyes of all healthy humans at the fresh age of ten minutes old. Marie-Claire looked up at me.

"*C'est ma fille. Ma chèrie fille.*" A tear escaped her eye.

"Yes, she's your dear daughter." Annie wiped away a tear from her own cheek.

"What will thee name her?" I asked, glad she'd birthed a girl. She might have grown to resent a male who would only remind her of his father.

She looked back down at the baby. "I should name her Verna, after her *Papa*. But I will not. She will be called Marie-Reine. She is a princess now, but she will rule her world when she is grown. No man will make her do anything she does not want to."

"It's a lovely name." I stood. "Annie will help thee with thy first suckling. I'll be back."

"Wait, Rose." Annie took me aside and whispered in my ear.

I narrowed my eyes and nodded once. "Very interesting." At her curious expression, I added, "I'll explain later." When I re-entered our sleeping car, I faced a crowd of female passengers even as a noise outside the window grew louder. Was this our rescue?

"Well?" one matron demanded. "Safe passage for the two?"

"Yes."

A girl piped up. "Is it a son or a daughter?"

I smiled. "A healthy baby girl and a healthy new mother."

A round of clapping subsided only when Spencer appeared at the end of the car, announcing, "The plow is coming!"

A cheer went up as I rushed to speak with him. "Spencer," I called.

He turned and waited until I caught up with him. "I need to inform all the cars. Can this wait?"

"No." I lowered my voice to a murmur. "I believe I found

evidence of poison in Vernon Peel's compartment. As soon as worldly possible, I need to speak with police."

He looked aghast. "Do you mean murder? On the Grand Trunk Line?"

"I do."

***

I led a ruddy-faced police officer to the café car. Once the track was clear, our train had proceeded as far as the nearest town, then waited while the authorities were fetched. I'd explained my find as well as what Annie had overheard. After their searches, they'd asked me to take them to the murderer.

Now I pointed to Eugenie. "Her."

"Miss Eugenie Villeneuve," the officer said, placing his hand on her shoulder. "We have reason to believe you caused the death of Mr. Vernon Peel."

The clatter of silverware and the buzz of conversation in the car hushed. All eyes were on the stern-faced maid.

Eugenie's face went as white as her collar. "I most certainly did not."

"The bartender has confirmed that you brought a last cup of rum punch to Mr. Peel in his berth last evening. The cup left at his feet has the distinctive poisonous odor of digitalis, which can be fatal in large doses, particularly to people with heart disease. And we have located Mr. Peel's vials of that same medicine in your own luggage."

Would he mention what Annie had told me, which I'd passed on to the officer, that she'd heard Eugenie muttering in French to herself in the café car when she'd gone to fetch the water? The maid had been thanking God for digitalis.

She pushed to standing and spit out a stream of French I could only assume were curse words I hadn't yet learned. She switched to English, her face now aflame. "He was an awful man. He abused Madame. He tried to force himself on me, too, but I fought him off. He deserved to die!"

"Miss Villeneuve, you are under arrest for the murder of Mr. Peel." He snapped handcuffs on her and led her away.

I supposed the police would question Marie-Claire as to whether she had put Eugenie up to the murder. I prayed that the new mother, who'd discovered joy with her baby, was innocent and that her maid had acted alone.

The silence, no longer ominous, disappeared as the train began to rumble and clatter once again toward Montreal.

The Unfortunate Death of Mrs. Edna Fogg

Author Note: When I realized November, 1888 was a Presidential election year, I knew I wanted to write about women's suffrage, since Quaker women had long been in the forefront of the movement. This story led to the third Quaker Midwife novel, *Turning the Tide.*

As I cycled home in the November dawn after safely delivering a baby, I hadn't expected to encounter a dead body. It was the red shoe sticking out from where no shoe should be that caught my eye, its color echoing the frost-burnished leaves of the lilac bush above it.

I let my bicycle fall to the side and hurried to the shrub. Pulling back the branches, my heart a-thudding, I gasped when I saw that the shoe was on the black-stockinged foot of Edna Fogg. I pulled off my glove and knelt to touch the neck of the well-known women's suffragist, a lady in her thirties. Her skin was cold and yellow, and not from the chilly fall air, either.

Poor Edna. I didn't know her well, but I'd always admired her fortitude in speaking out for a woman's right to vote, much as my own mother did. Edna wasn't a Quaker like we were, but she embodied our values of equality and integrity. I sniffed, picking up a scent other than dried leaves and wood smoke, but I couldn't identify it. Perhaps it was a perfume Edna used.

How had she died? Surely it wasn't from natural causes, not

with her ending up under a bush. I ran my gaze over her body. I saw no bullet hole or stab wound. I wanted to investigate further—perhaps she had an injury on her back or her head—but I knew from my encounters with him that Detective Kevin Donovan of the Amesbury Police Department would need to see her *in situ*. My eyes widened as I glimpsed a slip of paper tucked into Edna's hand.

I perked my ears at the sound of an approaching horse clopping along the cobblestones. It pulled an open buggy, and I stepped into the street, signaling the driver to stop.

"Excuse me, but a lady has died," I said to the driver. "Can thee please hurry to the police station and ask for Detective Donovan to come?"

"And why not the funeral parlor, miss?" The gentleman was about fifty. "If she's dead, as you say."

How much to tell him? "Please, I believe the police are needed in this case." I clasped my hands in front of me. Despite being half his age, I used my most authoritative voice and stood tall into my five feet eight inches.

He shrugged. "Very well." He clucked to the horse and clattered away.

I returned to Edna's side and closed my eyes, holding her released spirit in the Light of God. I also held my own, still very much of this world. I am a midwife, not a detective, and am accustomed on occasion to witnessing the unavoidable death of one of my mothers or newborns. But why did I keep encountering cases of violent death?

***

An hour later I sat in Bertie Winslow's cheery kitchen. I sipped the coffee she'd poured, inhaled the cinnamon-laden air, and continued to tell her the events of the morning. We'd worked together on several murder cases in the past, strictly as amateurs, of course, and I'd found I had something of a gift for investigation.

I knew my good friend, the unconventional postmistress of our bustling mill town, would be willing to discuss this death with me.

"Kevin appeared with several other officers," I said. "As usual, he looked askance at me but thanked me for raising the alarm. And for pointing out the paper in Edna's hand."

"And then kindly told you to absent yourself, I assume?" A wry grin pulled at Bertie's mouth.

"Indeed. Although not before I witnessed him raising Edna's head and discovering a great bloody wound on the back of it."

"Poor Edna." Her eyes went wide. "So somebody whacked her to death."

"It appears so, although Kevin did caution me against mentioning the method, so thee'll have to keep that information under thy hat." I frowned. "Bertie, I know thee must get along soon to open the post office. But I was much disturbed by finding Edna Fogg's body, and I thought thee might have known her better than I."

Bertie cocked her head of curly blond hair. "I've always admired Edna's suffrage work." She peered into a mirror on the wall, her expression somber, and pinned on one of her fanciful hats at her usual rakish angle. She turned back to face me. "Did you hear she recently left her husband of many years?"

"No. I know nothing of her personal life. Does thee know why she left Mr. Fogg? Was he cruel to her, or—"

Bertie held up her hand. "I'm not sure why she left. I do know she went to live with Frannie Murphy, another suffragist. I'll have to ask Sophie what the nature of their friendship is, since she and Edna are both lawyers." Sophie and Bertie lived together in what would have been called a marriage if one of them had been a man. "I daresay Hiram Fogg wasn't a bit happy about the move," she added.

"I would imagine not. Does she have children?"

"I don't believe so."

"And what is his chosen profession? Is he also in the law?"

"No." She pursed her lips. "I believe he's a physician."

"I wonder what the paper I saw was. Surely not a suicide note. Perhaps it was a warning of some kind." I glanced at the clock as I finished my coffee. "Thee needs to go. And I must rest before my afternoon appointments. I didn't sleep more than dozing during the early stages of my client's labor last evening."

We walked out together, and she mounted her horse, Grover. She'd named him after our president, an act completely in character with Bertie's irreverent nature. I waved goodbye and mounted my steel steed for the short ride home. Had Edna been equally as unconventional as Bertie and entered into a loving relationship with another woman? Perhaps Hiram Fogg had felt an irrational rage at being abandoned, especially for a woman, and had killed his wife. I'd have to see what I could learn, with the sole intent of assisting Kevin in his investigation, naturally.

***

Before my first pregnant client of the afternoon, I took a moment to pen a note to my mother. I jotted down pleasantries, inquired if she knew Edna Fogg from their mutual suffrage work, and told her about the death. I asked if she knew anything that might help in the investigation. Mother supported my talents in tracking down murderers. I sealed the envelope and set it out for the postman.

After my last client left at three o'clock, I sat and thought. Where could I learn more about both Hiram Fogg and Frannie Murphy, not to mention Edna? Bertie had said Edna was a lawyer, but I didn't know where she practiced. I snapped my fingers. I had a home visit scheduled later today. And Nan Pollard's husband was a lawyer.

Twenty minutes later Nan, cradling her eight-month-pregnant belly under sprigged fabric that strained at her full bosom, ushered me into an airy and spacious bedroom on Hillside Avenue.

"Will this do, Rose?" she asked, waving her arm to encompass the space. A four-poster bed draped with creamy brocade curtains held a position of honor. Two upholstered armchairs nestled near the east-facing window and a marble-faced fireplace was tucked into the opposite wall. Nan smoothed chestnut-colored hair off her brow, with a faint whiff of violet.

"It will do quite nicely, Nan." I made home visits to every client, whether the wife of a mill owner or the young mill worker, herself. I thought it passing odd Nan had even asked, since she'd given birth here twice before.

"My maid will bring you whatever you need," Nan said with a calm smile. "Mr. Pollard says to summon the carriage should we need a doctor in attendance."

I'd assisted at her prior births as an apprentice, but I was confident in being the lead midwife this time around. "I doubt we'll need a physician, Nan. Thy previous births were quite easy, as I recall."

Her brows knit together. "Mr. Pollard is very much in favor of having a male doctor attend me. But I don't agree, and I've put my foot down. The birthing chamber is the realm of women, is it not?"

I smiled and stroked her arm. "I believe it is, Nan. And I will take good care of thee." It was an honest answer. But how was I going to raise the issue of what George Pollard might know about Edna Fogg? As it happened, I didn't need to.

"Rose," Nan lowered her voice. "I heard Mrs. Fogg was killed. And that you found her body this morning. Is it true?" Her eyes were wide.

"Let's sit for a moment." I led her to the chairs by the window. Talk of murder wasn't exactly the calming topic one would wish for a near-term mother-to-be. After we sat, I went on. "I did find her, sadly. I was returning at dawn from a birth."

"Mr. Pollard said she was bashed in the back of the head. What a terrible death." She brought her hands to cover her mouth.

"Any violent death is a terrible one. I believe Edna was a lawyer, like thy husband. Was George acquainted with her?"

Nan's nostrils flared. "Acquainted? Why, she stole his job!" Nan suddenly looked neither surprised nor saddened about Edna's death.

That was quite the accusation. "How so?" I kept my expression even, despite my keen interest in learning more about this story.

"They're both employed by Bixby & Batchelder, or were. When my George was up for promotion, they chose that woman instead." She nearly spat the word *woman*. "And sacked Mr. Pollard." The anger slid off her face and sorrow crept into her voice. "Just like what happened to my Papa when I was a girl. He was a wrecked man after that."

"I'm so sorry, Nan. I trust George will find a new position soon."

"Maybe, if people about town stop laughing behind his back. And then Mrs. Fogg ups and leaves her own husband high and dry. There's just no decency in this world, Rose. What have we come to?"

***

At a few minutes before seven that evening, Bertie and I walked briskly toward the Free Will Baptist Church on Friend Street. She'd stopped by after supper and convinced me to attend a suffrage meeting with her.

"They're planning to start with tributes to Edna Fogg," Bertie said, tucking her arm through mine. "I thought you'd be interested."

"I wonder what her suffragist friends will say. One of my clients, Nan Pollard, told me her husband was passed over for a promotion in favor of Edna, and that the firm let him go. Nan seemed quite incensed about it."

Bertie snorted. "Sophie always says Pollard isn't exactly a Philadelphia lawyer."

I raised my eyebrows at the phrase. As a Quaker, I might interpret Philadelphia lawyer as one who embodied Friends' values rather than one with a keen intellect.

"Edna was smarter than him," Bertie went on. "I'm glad Mr. Batchelder recognized that."

"It's still quite rare for a woman to push ahead of a man like that." I glanced at Bertie as we arrived at the door. "Well, except for thee, of course." Bertie'd had quite a struggle to be appointed to her position as postmistress.

Inside, the hall was full of women, many seated, some conferring in small groups standing around the edges.

Bertie nudged me and made a small gesture toward a woman near us. "That's Frannie Murphy," she murmured. She hailed Frannie, who walked over.

Frannie was tall, not much older than I. She wore a mannish jacket over her black dress, with her auburn hair pulled back severely into a coiled braid.

"Frannie, I'm awfully sorry about Edna," Bertie said. "Rose here is a bit of a detective, you know."

"Rose Carroll." Frannie stared at me. "I heard you found my dear Edna. Was it a terrible sight? Do you think she suffered?"

I took her hand in both of mine. "I'm afraid I cannot say. But the detective told me she suffered a grievous head wound, so perhaps she lost consciousness immediately." I hoped that would console her.

"Who would harm such a graceful and brilliant person?" she whispered. "Such a loving soul?"

Bertie looked sympathetic. "I heard she was living with you."

Frannie took a deep breath in and let it out. "Yes. She couldn't tolerate that husband of hers any longer. Hiram is an ogre, and I invited her to share my flat." She looked intently at Bertie. "Edna wanted only a platonic friendship with me, and even that was so rich, so full. Yet she spoke of moving on again...." She pressed her lips together and shook her head, fast. "I mustn't dwell on it any longer. The suffrage movement needs me. And I have my memories."

Two women edged past us trailing a cloud of lavender. Frannie gave a low, sad laugh. "Edna would have been sneezing her head off at that smell. She had the worst reaction to scents."

An older lady walked to the front of the room and clapped several times. "The meeting of the Amesbury chapter of the Woman Suffrage Association will now come to order." She rapped a gavel on the table as Bertie and I made our way to two emptyseats.

So Hiram Fogg was an ogre, at least according to Frannie, who had possibly been in love with Edna. And Edna had talked about moving on. I had much to consider.

***

"Kevin, I'm assuming Edna Fogg's death was murder, since a blow to the back of the head couldn't be suicide," I said the next morning. I stood in front of the detective's desk in the police station, where the smell of stale cigar smoke mixed with the aroma of old wood and the coconut scent of the Macassar oil Kevin used on his hair. "And the death could hardly be accidental, with her lying under a lilac bush. I've obtained information thee might find useful in thy investigation."

"Now, Miss Rose. I hope you haven't been trying to play private detective again." He cocked his head and gave a scolding look.

I bristled inwardly at his choice of verbs, but kept my annoyance to myself. "I've merely collected some facts which could shed light on Edna's life and motivations. I'll leave, naturally, if thee has already made an arrest in the case."

He let out a noisy breath. "Surely you know I haven't, although I have located a possible witness to the crime."

"Excellent. What was on that piece of paper she held?"

"It was a handwritten note, asking her to meet at that spot."

"Not signed?" I asked.

"Sadly, no." He gestured at the chair. "Sit down, then, and tell me what you have."

"First, Edna had left her husband. She was living with the suffragist Frannie Murphy."

"Mr. Fogg told us she'd moved out, but not where." Kevin frowned. "That Murphy woman is a rabble-rouser of the highest order. What was a lovely lady like Mrs. Fogg doing with the likes of her?"

"I believe they were friends and shared a passion for a woman's right to vote." I watched him. "As does my mother, and I, myself."

"Regardless, I'm going to be looking hard at this Miss Murphy." He sighed. "Go on, please."

I ticked off the items on my fingers. "Second, last night Frannie told us—"

"Who's us?"

"Bertie Winslow took me to the suffrage meeting. Frannie told us Edna was talking about moving on again. She didn't say where. Frannie herself seemed quite broken up about Edna's death. I believe Edna might have disappointed Frannie in the, uh, scope of their friendship."

He looked up, shocked. "You mean...oh, never mind." He grabbed a stub of a pencil and scribbled on a piece of paper.

"Third, yesterday I was with a pregnant client of mine, Nan Pollard. She said the law firm of Bixby & Batchelder recently promoted Edna over Nan's husband, George. They let George go from the firm. Nan was quite incensed about that, and about Edna's leaving Hiram."

"As well she might be," Kevin murmured, staring at his notes.

At my exclamation, he glanced up and cringed. "Sorry, I was thinking out loud. Of course there's nothing wrong with a lady lawyer earning her keep, Miss Rose. But marriage vows—well, don't you think they should mean something?"

***

I had several prenatal appointments after I returned home, but the whole time my mind was half-occupied by thoughts of Edna's murder. The afternoon post arrived at two, with a return note from Mother. After greetings and bits of news about the Lawrence farm—Daddy's business, not hers—she wrote:

> *I met Edna Fogg at the April meeting where we founded the International Council of Women. She spoke even then about leaving her husband. He wanted them to raise a family, and that was not her chosen path. She dreamed of becoming a famous lawyer and planned to pursue that passion. Thee knows, my dear Rose, we women are not all suited for the life of wife and mother, despite thy calling to assist women in achieving exactly that.*

So that was why Edna had left Hiram. Even though I hoped for children of my own one day, I agreed with Mother: not all women wanted to bear children, for various reasons. If they didn't, their choice was the difficult one of ceasing intimate relations with their husbands.

And perhaps the pressure of Frannie's feelings for her was the reason Edna had mentioned moving on again. Last night Frannie had seemed sincere in her grief for Edna—but Frannie could have killed her because Edna had spurned the younger woman's love. Frannie might simply be a good actress. She was tall, young, and strong enough to strike a fatal blow to Edna's head. It was well that Kevin said he'd be looking into Frannie.

I finished reading and refolded the missive, thinking all the while. What about Hiram? I needed to learn more about Edna's husband. Bertie'd said he was a physician. I could pay my beau, David, a visit at his office at the hospital. I shook my head. No, I couldn't—he was away at a medical convention.

Or the killer could have been George Pollard, furious at losing his job to a woman. I had time to call at the law firm where George had worked. Someone might be willing to talk to me about him. Yes, I'd walk downtown to Bixby & Batchelder—

My thinking was interrupted by a loud rapping on the front door. A driver handed me a note. It read, in a flowing, educated hand:

Please come quickly. My pains have begun. Nan Pollard.

Good heavens. I made a quick calculation. She still had a month before the baby was due. I prayed the infant would be mature enough to sustain its passage out into the world and survive.

"I'm to take you to the Pollard home, miss," the driver said.

I checked the sky, cloudless and not too cold, with the sun still hanging above the horizon. "Thank thee, but I'll come along in a few minutes on my bicycle. I need to get my things together. Please have the maid put a large pot of water on to boil."

He tipped his hat and hurried back to the carriage.

I grabbed a piece of bread and a wedge of cheese and munched on them as I checked my birthing satchel. Labors were so unpredictable in length and intensity, I'd learned to snatch sustenance when I could. Cloaked, bonneted, and gloved, with my satchel strapped to the platform on the back of my cycle, I mounted and rolled down the hill.

Whether it was from the movement of the wheels or the intensity of the past two days I wasn't sure, but the last piece of the Edna puzzle fell into place in my brain as I rode. My eyes wide,

I detoured to the police station, pedaling like a madwoman, my eyeglasses sliding down the bridge of my nose.

I dashed up the steps of the station only to learn that Kevin wasn't in. I slapped the scarred wooden surface of the front desk in frustration.

"There's no need for that, miss," the young officer said.

"I apologize. I need to leave the detective a note, then. And thee must see that he gets it with all due dispatch." I stood tall and fixed my gaze on him. "It regards the recent murder."

He stared at me, but recovered enough to say, "Yes, miss."

***

The distraught young maid pulled open the door to the Pollard home. "Oh, Miss Carroll, I'm glad you've come. She's up there a-screaming."

"Don't worry thyself. It's what women do. I'll attend to her shortly. Are the children about?"

"No. Mrs. Pollard told Nursey to take them to their grandmother's."

"Good. I have a question for thee before I go up." I conferred with her until a cry of pain drifted down from upstairs. "Please put that item aside for me. And bring up hot water as soon as possible." I ran up the stairs.

"Where have you been, Rose?" Nan wailed from her bed as soon as I walked in. Her face was flushed and the hair around her forehead curly and damp.

"I'm here now, Nan." I cleaned my hands at the washstand and set out my birthing supplies. "When did the pains begin, and how far apart are they?"

"A couple of hours ago. They're getting closer and closer." As a contraction set in, Nan cried out again.

"Now, now," I said. "Blow out thy breath gently. If thee becomes tense, thy body will have more difficulty letting the baby come out." This was her third labor. She should have learned how to give birth by now, but perhaps she was afraid of bringing another baby into a family suddenly without a breadwinner.

***

Three hours later, as I was settling Nan and her tiny but healthy baby girl onto fresh pillows, I heard a commotion and shouting downstairs. Nan and I exchanged a look. The voices quieted and a moment later there was a rapping at the bedroom door.

I pulled it open to see a red-faced George Pollard, with Kevin right behind him.

"I've got to talk with Mrs. Pollard," her husband said. "She'll tell this fool I was right here the whole time!"

Kevin, still behind him, shook his head ever so slightly at me.

Nan called out, "Mr. Pollard, come see your daughter."

"A daughter? Our first girl?" He rushed toward the bed. He knelt to stroke the tiny newborn's head, and then his wife's cheek.

Kevin cleared his throat. "This is all very nice. But I'm afraid I'm here on official police business, as Mr. Pollard well knows." He turned to me and murmured, "May I speak with the newly delivered mother?"

"I think thee'd better." I raised my eyebrows.

"Please step away from the bed, Mr. Pollard," Kevin said.

George glared at him but obliged.

"Rose, will you fetch me my wrapper?" Nan pointed to the armoire.

I hurried over. When I opened the door, the scent of violets flooded my nostrils. I sniffed as I narrowed my eyes and stared at the hanging dresses without seeing them.

"Please, Rose?" Nan called. "I need to be decent with this policeman in the room."

I grabbed the wrapper and shut the door. Nan handed the baby to George before donning the garment. Kevin approached the couple.

"Mrs. Pollard," Kevin began. "Where was your husband Sunday night between dusk and approximately five o'clock in the morning?"

"Why, he was right here with me, Officer. Weren't you, dear?"

George kept his eyes on the baby in his arms and nodded.

"Nan, on Monday thee told me Edna had been bashed in the head," I said. "Thee had no way of knowing that. Right, Kevin?"

"That is correct. You, Miss Rose, were the only person outside of the police to see that. And we made quite sure not to let that fact slip out to the newspapers."

"Why, I heard it somewhere," Nan scoffed, tossing her head. "The news must have gotten around town. I think the maid told me."

"I don't believe so. In fact, on Second Day thee said George told thee about the bashing." I turned to Kevin. "The maid is downstairs, and she's holding a shirt of George's that has bloodstains on it."

"Cut myself with the razor, that's all it was." George turned his scowl in my direction. A tic beat near his lip and sweat popped out on his forehead like nervous pearls.

"Nan, it pains me to say this," I said, "but thee helped kill Edna, didn't thee?"

"How dare you!" His nostrils flaring, George took a step toward me.

"Hand me the baby." I held out my arms. "She's very small and will not tolerate thy anger." To my surprise he obliged.

"Mrs. Pollard had nothing to do with it," George blustered. "She was home the whole night!"

"No, she wasn't," I continued. "Nan, I smelled the scent of violets when I found Edna's body. That's thy perfume."

"I'm not the only lady who wears violet!" She made as if to climb out of bed, but George put his hand on her shoulder. "Edna must have fancied the same aroma."

I smiled sadly. "Frannie Murphy said Edna had a severe sneezing reaction to scents. No, that was thee, luring her to that house with the note, pushing George to kill her. Thee couldn't stand that she was given his job."

"Well, it was neither fair nor right. And you don't have any proof of anything. Now give me my baby." She extended her arms.

I shook my head. With my unoccupied hand I drew the note the driver had brought me out of my pocket. "Kevin, I think if thee compares the handwriting on this note with the one found at the body, they will be identical."

"Officers?" Kevin called out as he took the note and thanked me with his eyes. Two policemen hurried in.

"We interviewed a witness who places you both, Mr. and Mrs. Pollard, at the scene of the crime Sunday evening at seven o'clock." Kevin laid a hand on George's arm, a move I'd learned was required by the police at the time of an arrest. "George Pollard, you are under arrest for the murder of Mrs. Edna Fogg." The men moved toward George. He cast an anguished look at his wife but didn't struggle as an officer ushered him out.

Kevin reached down and lightly touched Nan's shoulder. She twisted away. "Nanette Pollard, you are under arrest as an accessory to the murder of Mrs. Edna Fogg. I'll call for a police matron to stay with you until you are recovered enough to be transported to the jail."

"You can't do that!" She gazed at her baby with stricken eyes, as if only now realizing the impact of her crime. She brought her hand to her mouth as tears seeped from her eyes.

"Indeed I can." He instructed the other officer to fetch the matron. Kevin turned to me. "Thank you," he whispered.

I acknowledged his appreciation with a frown. I was getting better at detecting, true. I gazed at the sweet warm bundle in my arms. She and her brothers would now be no different than orphans due to the desperate, foolish actions of their parents. I'd helped justice to be served, but at a tragic cost. Perhaps I should stick to midwifery from now on.

Murder in the Summer Kitchen

Author Note: During my time writing the Rose Carroll novels and short stories, I trained as a docent in the John Greenleaf Whittier home museum. Many nineteenth-century homes included a summer kitchen separate from the main house, which both kept the house cooler and reduced risk of fire. I wrote this story for an anthology to benefit the Whittier Birthplace, a homestead museum in the neighboring city of Haverhill.

In the gloaming of the Eleventh Month afternoon, my attention had wandered from the literary conversation in John Greenleaf Whittier's parlor. The unmistakable crack of a gun brought me to my senses, and I jumped in my seat. Another report followed in quick succession.

All the eyes in the room went wide along with mine: John's, my niece Faith's, those of several other Friends, and Celia Thaxter's, John's famous colleague whose work we were here to discuss. Faith clutched my hand. A man named Zachariah leaped to his feet.

"What violence is this?" he cried.

The unflappable Celia raised an eyebrow. "Sounded like a gun to me." While not a Quaker, her dress was fully as plain as mine, although hers was adorned with a necklace made from seashells.

It had sounded like a gun to me, too. I'd witnessed the discharge of weapons on more than one occasion, and most of those times were not happy ones.

John tented his fingers. "Young ruffians sometimes prowl the streets of late. 'Tis a pity they cannot rightly be controlled by their parents." His high brow wrinkled in disapproval.

Mrs. Cate, John's housekeeper, clattered down the stairs from the quarters she kept with her husband, the Judge, and appeared in the doorway. "You're all right then, Mr. Whittier?"

"Yes, Mrs. Cate. Does thee know whence came this gunshot?" He stroked his snowy-white chinstrap beard.

"I do believe it was from the summer kitchen." She hugged herself, her mouth drawn down. "But why?"

"I'll go to investigate," Zachariah said. He was no taller than my five feet eight, nor much older than my twenty-four years.

"I'll come with thee," I said, standing.

"What has a midwife to do with guns?" Zachariah's eyes scoffed under sand-colored eyebrows.

"Rose Carroll is not only a midwife, young man." John came to my defense. "She's also something of a detective."

***

A few moments later Zachariah and I stood in the small outbuilding to the side of the house. Calling it a summer kitchen was a misnomer, since Mrs. Cate cooked in it year-round except in deep midwinter. No food preparation would take place here this evening, though. A man lay on his side on the wooden floor with his back toward us. Even in the twilight I could see a dark ragged hole piercing his back. Blood stained his jacket and the floor beneath.

I pushed past Zachariah and knelt, feeling the man's neck. His skin was still warm, but his pulse was gone. I reached over his head and smoothed his eyelids shut before standing. I shivered, from the sight of another violent death as much as from the cold.

"Does thee know this man?" I asked.

Zachariah shook his head. "Never seen him before."

"Why, that's our handy boy," Mrs. Cate's voice came from

behind me. "That's Mr. Price. John Price does odd jobs around the house and garden, don't you know. I daresay he was come to empty the ashes from the stove, just like I'd asked him to." She held a lit oil lantern high.

The light showed that, indeed, an ash bucket lay on its side near the man's feet.

I turned to Mrs. Cate. "Was he a surly man, likely to have enemies?"

"Oh, no, Miss Carroll. He was the sweetest fellow," she said. "Almost too sweet, if you get my meaning. A bit simple in the head, but an excellent worker. Quite trustworthy."

"Zachariah, thee must fetch Detective Kevin Donovan." I frowned. "He'll need to begin his investigation."

Zachariah pursed his lips and frowned back. "Very well," he finally said, and made his way out.

Mrs. Cate set the lantern on top of the table and reached for the victim's shoulder as if to turn him. "We'll need to set this fellow to rights."

I grabbed her hand. "No, we shouldn't touch him."

She glanced at me in alarm. "And why ever not?"

"The police will want to see him exactly as he fell. They'll make a determination of where the shot was fired from and perhaps gain other evidence as to the identity of the murderer. I'll stay here. Thee can return to the house if thee likes."

"A young woman like you stay with a dead man alone? Why, I never. What if that killer comes back? No, I'll stay here with you."

In my profession as a midwife, I was not unfamiliar with death. In my recent investigations of murder in our town, I'd found a source of bravery in myself that had surprised me. Still, I didn't argue with her. It was a comfort to have the matronly woman at my side, even if she wasn't exactly an armed guard.

***

Twenty minutes later I was safely back in the parlor relating the details about both scene and victim to the gathering. "Kevin, the lead detective in the local police, arrived with several of his men and shooed us out. He'll handle the case from here on."

"He is an able investigator, our Kevin." John studied me. "But, Rose, I am seized with an unfortunate idea."

I waited for him to go on, imagining the workings of his creative brain, a mind which had produced so many lyrical poems. Celia cocked her head, stroking the head of a figure on one of the plaster scenarios of the Civil War that had been gifts to John in thanks for his abolitionist work.

"What idea would that be, Mr. Whittier?" the well-known author, poet, and artist asked. She was robust of figure, with an inquisitive face and curly white hair worn in a knot on top of her head.

Faith sat up straight, gazing at Celia. My seventeen-year-old niece, with her own dreams of becoming a widely read author, had been excited at John's invitation to meet his good friend.

"Thee might not know, dear Celia, that I am in the habit of making my own tea in the summer kitchen of an afternoon," John said. "Mrs. Cate works tirelessly all day long and I don't wish to bother her for my hot drink. What if –"

"The shooter mistook John Price for thee?" I asked. My heart chilled at the thought of losing this avuncular friend, this Friendly mentor, this national treasure. "In truth the late-day light at this time of year is quite dim, with the sun leaving us well before five o'clock. And he was a tall, thin man, much like thyself."

"Exactly my thoughts, Rose," John said. "And he shot the wrong John."

"But surely thee doesn't have enemies," Faith said. "Who would want to kill thee?"

John gave her a kindly look. "The human species has capacity for hurt feelings that far exceeds reason, my dear. Those who fought to keep the institution of slavery alive only two-some decades ago still harbor ill will against we who worked to destroy it. Also, some of the many fans of my little poems have expressed outrage that I cannot meet with them personally."

Celia rose and adjusted the array of late fall flowers and colorful leaves she'd arranged in a vase on the mantel. "An artist has only so much strength for such encounters, I agree." She nodded. "We must conserve our energies for our work."

***

"But Rose, ain't it too early?" Prissy Gund said at seven the next morning as her latest pain ebbed. "My baby ain't supposed to come for another couple of weeks. Didn't you tell me that?" She flopped back on the bed pillows.

"A few weeks doesn't make much difference, Prissy," I said, smiling in what I hoped was a reassuring way. "The baby should be big enough to survive by now, and thee might have an easier time of the birth since your child will be a little smaller than at term."

My young apprentice, Annie Beaumont, and I had been at Prissy's small cottage in Patten Hollow for two hours now, after Willard Gund had come to fetch me in the dark hours of the First Day morning. Annie, a good friend of Faith's, had quit her job at the Hamilton Mill to apprentice with me, and I welcomed her assistance. The bedroom was small but clean. Willard had brought us basins and a kettle of recently boiled water.

"You'll take good care of my Prissy, won't you?" the first-time father asked me, looking both tender and terrified.

"Of course we shall, Willard. Thee is not to worry. I'll bring thee news of thy baby as soon as the birth is safely accomplished."

He thanked me, wringing his hands. He planted a kiss on his wife's forehead, then left the bedchamber with a panicked look on his face.

"He just can't wait for our little one," Prissy said. "I've never seen him so excited about anything."

Now Annie wiped Prissy's brow as I picked up the Pinard horn to listen to the baby's heart. "Let me listen to the heartbeat for a moment while thee is in between pains," I said.

The fetal heartbeat was strong and regular, an excellent sign.

"I want my mama," Prissy wailed as another contraction set in. But her mother was in far northern Maine. Prissy herself had recently been a mill girl until Willard offered her marriage and a modest living on his carriage factory wages.

I checked the watch pinned to my chest. Only two minutes had passed since the previous contraction. This baby would be along soon.

"I'll assess thy dilation after this pain."

Annie perched on the edge of the bed holding Prissy's hand. "You're going to be fine, Prissy," she murmured. "Try not to become tense."

I smiled. Annie had a naturally soothing manner about her even at eighteen. For a moment my thoughts flashed back to the poor man on John Whittier's kitchen floor. No one would ever soothe him again.

After Prissy quieted again, I slid my hand inside her and measured the opening with my knuckles. I removed my hand and wiped it clean.

"Thy baby is almost here, Prissy. Take some deep breaths now while thee can. Thee will feel the urge to push soon, and we'll want thee to." I stood and checked the folded linens on the dresser next to a cross on a stand. I beckoned to Annie. "See if thee can find Willard. We'll need more than these two cloths."

Annie nodded. She glanced at Prissy, who was resting with eyes closed. "I heard about the body at Mr. Whittier's," Annie whispered to me. "That you found it."

"I did."

"What's this about Mr. Whittier?" Prissy called.

The mother-to-be suddenly had very acute hearing and I was sorry she'd overheard us.

"It's nothing, Prissy," I said, moving to her side. I motioned to Annie to go.

She set to groaning, a deep sound from her very core.

"Sit up a bit," I said, helping her farther up in bed. "Grab thy knees with thy hands and push."

Her face reddened with the effort and the groaning turned to an animal sound very much like a growl. When she was spent, she flopped back against the pillows and shut her eyes.

"Very good," I said. "A few more like that and you can meet your son or daughter."

"My husband hates Mr. Whittier," she murmured. "Despises him."

I narrowed my eyes. "Why, pray tell?"

"Willard's from North Carolina, and his family...ooh..." Prissy grabbed her knees again and produced another long guttural sound.

I couldn't pay attention to my roiling thoughts, but I wanted to. A Southern husband who hated John? I hadn't noticed Willard's accent, but maybe he'd come to the North when he was a child. What if he– *Not now, Rose.*

I knelt on the end of the bed. Her opening was bulging and I caught sight of a smattering of dark hair, another good sign. But where was Annie? We were going to need those cloths, and soon.

When the contraction subsided, the top of the head slipped back out of view. "Prissy, with the next pain I want you to give a mighty push. Does thee hear me?"

"Yes," she said but her voice was faint.

I took a moment to close my eyes and hold her and her baby in the Light of God, that they would both survive this dangerous journey. True, women's bodies were designed to birth their young, but that didn't make it any easier for many, and babies often suffered in the process, as well.

Annie burst back in the room. "I can't find him anywhere," she muttered.

What if Willard had heard the name of his mistaken victim last night and had gone back to shoot John Whittier? My nostrils flared but I could do nothing about such a threat until Prissy's baby was safely born.

"Search the bureau for a clean chemise, a pillowcase, anything."

"Help me," Prissy wailed.

***

Help her, we did, and twenty minutes later a clean baby boy lay in the arms of her wide-eyed mother. Prissy gazed at her son and then up at me with full eyes.

"Ain't he beautiful?" she asked. "I want to show him to his papa." Her gaze fell back on the newborn and she stroked his cheek with her finger.

"I'll go and find him. Annie, thee stay with Prissy and help her with the first feeding."

Annie opened her mouth to speak, and then shut it, nodding. I wished I could explain my fear, but time did not permit.

***

I was completely out of breath from pedaling my safety bicycle like a Fury all the way uphill out of Patten's Hollow to John's home on Friend Street. I'd stopped at the police station and dashed in, but Kevin was not about. I told the young officer at the desk to find the detective and send him along to John Whittier's house with great dispatch. The bell at Saint Joseph's rang nine times as I passed the massive red-brick Catholic church.

Now I let my cycle drop at the back of John's house. I hurried to the summer kitchen, which was blessedly empty of bodies. The blood had been scrubbed from the floor and the stove was hot to the touch. Mrs. Cate would have prepared breakfast already and, as it was First Day, she and her husband had likely already left for their own worship services. I knew they were not members of the Society of Friends.

A horse snorted from Pickard Street at the side of the yard. I'd missed it when I arrived. My eyes widened to see it was the Gunds' dappled mare harnessed to their simple open buggy. I was right. Willard was here. My heart set to thumping against my rib cage.

It was nine o'clock, too early for John to have departed for Meeting for Worship, since the Meetinghouse was only a quarter mile down the road. Had Willard already killed him? How soon would Kevin arrive?

I crept up to the back door. Despite my gloves, fear had turned my hands icy, nearly numb. I managed to pull open the door without a sound. Voices drifted through the house from the direction of the parlor. I edged along the wall until I could peer in.

John and Celia sat side by side on the settee, with Willard pointing a gun straight at them. I barely kept from crying out.

"Now, young man," John said in a low and calming register. "Thee must lower thy weapon. We can discuss this matter in a peaceful fashion." He rested both hands on his silver-handled cane.

Willard shook his head, his dark eyes as wild as his thatch of unruly hair. He did not lower the gun. "No, we can't. You and your abolitionist friends ruined my family. We couldn't maintain our farm without no slaves. My daddy kilt hisself and my momma, she died of a broken heart. It's all your fault."

Celia sat back on the settee and folded her arms. "What good do you think it'll do to add two more murders to your list, Mr. Gund? You already killed the handy man, I hear. You shoot my friend Mr. Whittier and the law will see you hanged."

Willard glanced around quickly, like a trapped weasel. "I didn't mean to kill that fellow. I thought it was Mr. Whittier here!"

I stepped into the room. "Thee killed the wrong John, Willard."

Willard whipped his head toward me. "Miss Carroll, what're you doing here?"

"I wonder the same, Rose," John added.

A little smile played on Celia's face, but she didn't speak.

"Thee has a newborn boy," I said.

Willard's face broke into a broad smile. "I do? A son?" His voice rose with joy but his weapon stayed trained on John.

"Yes, but he's very poorly." I added the lie because I had to. "Thee must abandon thoughts of murder and rush to his side." I caught John's gaze, looked fixedly at his walking stick, and tried to give him an unspoken message.

"Poorly? That can't be," Willard exclaimed. "What do you mean?"

I moved into the room to his side. "He's ailing. Please go to him and thy wife. She needs thee."

The distraught father stared at John. Willard's face glistened and the air smelled of desperation. If he decided to complete his terrible mission, he'd likely kill all three of us. My throat thickened as I tasted fear. The next few seconds lasted a year. Willard slowly lowered his gun. I let out the breath I hadn't realized I was holding.

"I'll hold that," John said, extending one hand. "Thee wouldn't want to have a gun near a baby."

Willard handed John the butt of the weapon. Willard took two steps toward the door before John stuck out his cane – aiming it in front of Willard's feet. He tripped and sprawled face first, crying out as he went.

In one move I hoisted the heavy plaster statuette of a Southern woman and her babe and dropped it, shuddering as I did. I had to ensure Willard wouldn't rise in anger and attack John again. I'd aimed for Willard's head but the statuette fell onto his back and cracked into half a dozen pieces.

The front door crashed open. Kevin appeared in the hall with his weapon drawn. As the ruddy-faced officer took in the scene, he lowered the gun.

"Well, well, Miss Rose. Looks like you're not needing me after all."

"We'll certainly need you to throw this scalawag in the clink, Detective," Celia said with a wry smile.

Willard might have been a hopeful new father, but he was much more than a scalawag. My heart broke for poor Prissy, and for John Price's family, as well as for the unfortunate Willard himself. Justice, even when served, was rarely kind.

The Mayor and the Midwife

Author Note: The big mystery convention known as Bouchercon took place in New Orleans one year, and all stories submitted for the anthology had to have a connection to that fabulous city. I decided to bring NOLA to Amesbury. The insightful independent editor (and dear friend) Ramona DeFelice Long, who edited the first six Rose Carroll books before her death in 2021, was from that part of Louisiana. Always generous with writers, she posted a couple of essays on the language and culture of the area, from which I drew heavily for this story, which was nominated for in 2016 for an Agatha Award for Best Short Story.

A stylishly dressed young woman let herself out of the modest home where I, midwife Rose Carroll, was headed. As I approached my pregnant client's abode, the girl turned and we nearly collided.

"Pardon me, miss," she exclaimed before sweeping past. Her day gown, of a lawn fabric sprigged with tiny pink-and -red flowers, was cut in the new narrower style, with wide lace added at the neck and waist. Her flamboyant scarlet hat, worn at a jaunty angle nearly hiding her face, looked like one of the designs from Mrs. Hallowell's Millinery.

Amused by this devotion to fashion, one which I neither shared by nature nor was allowed to indulge in by my Quaker faith, I knocked at the door, above which hung a small brass Jesus on a cross. A maid showed me in.

The mother-to-be, Venice Shakspeare Currier, sat in her

bedroom cradling her well-rounded belly. A white candle flickered on a low table in the corner, where a small brocade rug invited kneeling to pray to a gilded image of the Virgin Mary.

After I greeted Venice, I said, "I passed thy caller in the lane just now." I unpacked a tape measure and Pinard horn from my birthing satchel.

"That was Addie Daigle," Venice replied. "She recently married my cousin Anton, who's my husband's business partner. It was sweet of her to stop in, since I'm certainly not going out these days."

I proceeded to measure her belly from top to bottom. I pressed the flared end of the horn against her taut skin and listened to a strong, rapid fetal heartbeat. "It's fine for thee to take some air in the lane."

"It's mild now. But, Miss Rose, I don't know how I'll care for my little fellow when winter comes. It's going to be awfully cold here in Massachusetts, isn't it?" This was the young wife's first year away from her family in New Orleans. She'd expressed to me on several occasions her apprehensions about having married Warren Currier and moving all the way from Louisiana to Amesbury. She didn't question her love for her husband, but she worried about the weather.

"Indeed, it will be quite cold this winter." I took her pulse.

"Warren tells me he's going to have to halt his steamboat excursions when the Merrimack River freezes over. I've never seen a river go solid." Her honey-colored eyes widened.

"Thee shouldn't worry. Thee will bundle thy child properly and thyself, as well."

"I'll try. Warren wants to name the baby Joseph after my papa. He's the mayor of New Orleans, you know," she boasted in a gentle tone, pronouncing the name of the city something like "Nah-linz."

"Thee knows we cannot discern before the birth if the child

will be male or female." I pushed my spectacles back up the bridge of my nose.

"*Mais oui,* of course." She smiled, then cast me a look. "You know, my grandfather speaks Quaker talk like you do."

"Really? Thy grandfather is a Quaker?"

"He is. *Grandpère* came to Louisiana all the way from Delaware," Venice said. "My papa doesn't talk the way you do, but he's a reformer because of what *Grandpère* taught him. Trying to fix politics in New Orleans isn't easy." Venice let out a long yawn.

"I'm going to let thee rest now. All seems well."

I let myself out. Warren Currier hadn't made an appearance, but he was no doubt at work in his steamboat office a mile away on the Merrimack. A native of Amesbury, he'd been apprenticing on a steam paddleboat on the Mississippi when he'd met and fallen in love with Venice.

I stepped out onto the lane. The afternoon sun on this lovely autumn day illuminated the red and golden leaves like a gilt-edged painting.

A fine Hollander rockaway carriage pulled up to the house, its high graceful wheels crunching on the paving stones. After the uniformed driver pulled the glossy brown Morgan horse to a halt, a man in a handsome suit and top hat stepped out of the coach, his dark moustache well oiled, his midsection well fed.

"Good afternoon, miss," he said, tipping his hat. "I'd be much obliged if you would show me into this fine abode." He widened the vowels like Venice did, with the middle of "obliged" and "fine" stretching into "ah" sounds. "If it is the home of a Mister Warren Currier, that is."

I extended my hand. "I'm Rose Carroll. This is indeed Warren's home, and that of his wife, Venice. But I'm not employed in the household. Thee will have to ask the maid for admittance."

The man stared at me for a moment, then threw his head back and laughed before shaking my slender hand with his meaty one.

"A Quaker, are you?" he exclaimed. "*Mon Dieu*, just like my dear *Papere*."

"I am, and a midwife, as well." I cocked my head. "Would thee happen to be Venice's father, come from New Orleans?"

"That's the truth, young lady. I'm Joseph Shakspeare. Has my grandson arrived yet?"

"Not yet. It could be another six weeks, although the baby will likely arrive in about a month's time."

"And how fares my girl?"

"Thy daughter is quite healthy."

"*Très bien*. Her mother sent me to check on Venice's welfare, as the Missus is involved with her own nursling. Our youngest of six is only a year old and quite attached yet to his meals of mother's milk."

"As it should be," I said. "Farewell, then. Enjoy thy stay."

He twirled one end of his moustache and regarded me. "*Mais*, I've just come from a visit with the selectmen of this fair town. Thought we could exchange some honest words about city government and all that, seeing as how I'm a mayor looking to reverse a terrible situation of corruption. But those fellows were *pas vaillant*. You know, standoffish."

"It is New England, land of the Puritans." I tried to suppress my smile. "And I know the term. I speak some French with my French-Canadian clients."

"Well, what's a man got to do to buy his colleagues a drink in this town?"

I thought for a moment. "I can introduce thee tomorrow to our town's police detective. Kevin Donovan is a competent and forthcoming officer. He'd be willing to talk with thee about government. He also enjoys a spot of drink."

"Splendid, my dear Quaker, splendid. Send word as to the time and I shall appear."

"I will, Joseph."

"*Merci.* Now I must find my Venice."

I was surprised to see tears well up in his eyes. He may have been a metropolitan mayor fighting corruption, but he was a tender one.

***

At nine o'clock the next morning I sat in Kevin's office with Joseph. He'd picked me up in the hired carriage and now we waited for Kevin to appear.

"Venice was happy to see thee yesterday, I'd guess," I said.

"Indeed she was." Joseph beamed. "We're going out on the river later today on Warren's pleasure boat, since the weather is so fine. We're going to pass a good time."

"It'll be a pleasant ride."

Kevin burst into the room mopping his high rounded brow with a handkerchief. "Pardon my tardiness, sir." He pumped Joseph's hand, then greeted me. "Hello, Miss Rose."

"Joseph, I'd like thee to meet Detective Kevin Donovan," I said. "Kevin, Joseph Shakspeare, mayor of New Orleans."

"Excellent to meet you, Detective. Miss Carroll here says you run a tight ship."

"We do our best." Kevin sat behind his messy desk. "But don't you mean Shakespeare, Miss Rose?" He cocked his head.

Joseph laughed. "Everyone thinks I can't spell my own name. No, Miss Carroll was correct. I share the Bard's name minus one letter."

"I see." Kevin nodded. "Now, what can I help you with, Mayor?"

"My mission is to reduce corruption in city government. We have a group called the Ring down there, and they oppose me at every turn. I'm here visiting my daughter, Mrs. Currier, and thought I'd see what the fine town of Amesbury had to offer."

"I will leave you gentlemen to it." I rose. "I'm off to see clients."

Both men also stood. Kevin opened his mouth to speak when a young officer appeared in the doorway. "Excuse me sir, but there's been a death near the Merrimack, a Warren Currier. The death might be suspicious."

I gasped. Not Venice's husband.

Joseph's eyes widened. "*Maudit!*" he whispered.

"Currier. That's your daughter's married name, you said?" a frowning Kevin asked Joseph.

"Her husband's Christian name is Warren." Joseph, his face pale, turned to the young officer. "He's a paddleboat owner. That the one?"

"Yes, sir."

I brought my hand to my mouth. Another suspicious death in our quiet town.

"This is a disturbing turn of events." Kevin shook his head.

"Has his wife been informed?" I asked. This kind of shock could easily bring on labor. Her baby might be mature enough by now to survive the birth, or might not.

"Not yet, ma'am," the officer said.

"I must go to her. My *pauvre fille*," Joseph said. "You'll come along, Miss Carroll?"

"Of course. Let me quickly pen a note to my next client saying I need to cancel. I can hail a boy outside to deliver it."

I looked at the detective. I'd assisted him in several cases by keeping my eyes and ears open in the community, especially in the bedchambers of my birthing women, where secrets were often revealed during their travails. The detective had reluctantly grown to accept my participation.

"If it's murder, I'd like to help by listening, watching, and reporting to thee as I have done in the past."

Kevin nodded. "Then meet me at the Currier steamboat dock after you see to the wife, will you?"

***

I climbed out of Joseph's carriage in front of the dock an hour later. He'd instructed the driver to take me down to the river. Before I'd left Venice's side I ascertained that, so far at least, the distraught young woman had not started her labor. I left her father to console her and said I'd be back.

The dock bustled with police. A coroner's wagon was parked nearby, its gray horse waiting patiently in the traces. The open upper deck of the long white steamboat, a deck I'd seen full of weekend frolickers recently, now sat empty and forlorn.

The door to a small building opened. Kevin and another officer walked out grasping a struggling young man between them.

"*Moi*, I never did!" the fellow exclaimed. "I wouldn't kill Warren. We're in business together." His speech lilted in the southern way like Venice's.

"Yes, but you're also employed sewing sails as a side business, I hear," Kevin said. "That puncture wound in the victim's neck could've come only from a needle, and I very much doubt it was self-inflicted." He caught sight of me. "Ah, Miss Rose. We're taking Anton Daigle in for questioning."

Anton's eyes pleaded with me. "I didn't kill *mon cousin*, miss. I didn't."

"Come along, now." Kevin and the other officer bundled Anton into the back of the police wagon parked behind the ambulance. As the door shut, Kevin turned back toward me, dusting off his hands.

"What reason would Anton have to kill his partner?" I asked.

"He probably had a deal where he'd inherit the victim's half of the business. Sometimes they write up contracts like that."

"Did thee find the murder weapon?"

"Not yet. I'll show you the body."

"Very well." As a midwife, I was acquainted with death, beyond the several murder victims I'd had the misfortune to encounter. I did my best to bring women and babies safely through the normal but dangerous journey of birth. But sometimes I lost a mother or a newborn, or an infant succumbed to disease in its first weeks. I'd seen lifeless bodies before.

I followed Kevin into the office building, barely more than a shack with a window where tickets were sold. A wooden desk faced the door and another lined the back wall.

Warren Currier lay half on his side behind the front desk. One hand grasped a tipped-over chair as if he'd reached for it as he fell. A dark pool soaked the floor under his neck and red marks slashed the side wall. An officer guarded the body.

"Watch the door from outside," Kevin instructed him. After the man left, Kevin moved the victim's head slightly and pointed. "See here? Stabbed in the neck. Daigle there knew exactly how to hit the vital vein."

I gathered my skirts in my hands to keep them away from the blood and leaned down to examine the neck. Indeed, a small round puncture wound pierced the skin above where Warren's right carotid artery would be. The spray on the wall would be from the pressure of the heart continuing to pump out blood until the poor man had lost enough to die.

"Looks like a needle wound, wouldn't you say?" Kevin asked.

"Certainly a thin sharp object. Thee hasn't found it?"

"Not yet, but we will."

"Who reported the death this morning?"

"It was Daigle himself." Kevin's mouth turned down in disgust. "A fellow worker said that Daigle had just arrived when he dashed back out and raised the alarm. Probably killed Currier earlier, went home for breakfast, and came back all calm and easy like."

"Of course thy officers will closely question the neighbors and other businesses here on the river." I stared at him over my spectacles. "Thee has a penchant for jumping to conclusions a bit too hastily, Kevin."

He cleared his throat. "Of course we will. And we'll find the bloody needle, too."

***

After they carried out Warren's body, and with Kevin's permission, I made my own search of the office. I pulled out desk drawers, knelt to peer under the furniture, and checked the dusty corners. I examined the ticket counter, with its used tickets stuck on a spike.

I didn't locate the weapon, however. I peered closely at the spike. While its tip was certainly sharp enough, the rest of it was too thick to have caused the small wound. The carotid rested about an inch and a half in from the skin of the neck, if I remembered my anatomy studies correctly. No, a long sharp needle or pin was going to be the culprit. Unfortunately, it could be deep in the river by now.

I did find one small item that seemed out of place in an office. I pocketed the slim white feather, thinking to pass it along to Kevin. Perhaps it wasn't suspicious. There were gulls and other birds aplenty along the wide river, still tidal here ten miles inland from the Atlantic. But the detective might want to take a look.

When I went outside, though, Kevin had left. The officer on guard said he'd gone back to the station. I began my walk back toward the grieving young widow. Could Kevin's posited motive could possibly be true?

***

"Boil water," I directed Venice's maid as a clock chimed noon. "And I'll need a stack of clean cloths and two basins." As I'd feared, Venice was experiencing regular and increasingly frequent pains of labor when I arrived. I was glad I'd left my birthing satchel here this morning before departing for the dock. Joseph paced in the back of the room.

He hurried to where I stood. "Did the detective figure out how Warren died?" he whispered.

"He appears to have been murdered," I murmured. "Kevin thinks it was your nephew Anton."

"*Quoi*?" Venice screeched. "Anton wouldn't kill my Zach."

"Anton said as much," I told her. "But the detective took him in for questioning, regardless."

Venice groaned as another contraction set in. "Thee must wait in another room," I said to Joseph. "I need to examine the baby's progress. And we can't be having a man in the birthing chamber."

He nodded. "Just one moment."

He knelt in the prayer corner, crossed himself as he bowed his head, then folded his hands in front of his chest. He murmured prayers for a minute, then crossed himself again.

"*Fait du mal!* It hurts, *Papere*," Venice wailed, her eyes squeezed shut and her face crunched in pain.

"*Cher*, you'll be all right." Joseph stood and stroked his daughter's forehead with a gentle hand, but he wore one of the most anguished faces I'd ever seen on a man. "I look forward to meeting *le petit*, and we're going to bring you and him home to *Maman* as soon as we can. Don't you worry about a little thing. Miss Rose here is going to take good care of you."

He left and the young maid returned, eyes wide. She placed the kettle on a dresser, setting the folded linens and basins next to it. "Do you need me to help, miss?"

I let out a breath. I very much wished to have an apprentice at my side, but the one I was training was away. "I should be fine. But please don't be far in case I call for thee."

She nodded and scurried out as Venice lay curled on the bed, moaning through another pain.

When her contraction ended, I said, "I need thee to sit up." I propped pillows at the head of the bed and boosted her up until she was sitting almost straight. "Bend thy knees. I'm going to check the opening to thy womb."

"I want my *défunt* Zach." She gazed at me, tears streaming down her face. "My baby won't have a *Papere*, Rose. Whatever will I do?"

"Thee has a caring father and family back home. But let's get this baby out first."

I washed my hands, wishing I could also wash away this dire situation. A baby coming too early, a murdered father, and a mother far away from anything familiar.

I pushed up the sleeve of my gray work dress and slid my hand inside her. Only a half-knuckle's worth of dilation remained. I slid my hand out as I held her and the baby in a moment of silent prayer, that they would both make it through the next hour in good health.

With her next pain, Venice grabbed her knees, emitting a guttural sound. When the contraction subsided, she collapsed back on the pillows. "Rose, I'm afraid. Some *bon de rien* killed my husband. Am I next?"

It was my turn to stroke her sweaty brow. "There, there. No bad person's coming to kill thee."

"Anton never would've hurt Zach. His wife, Addie? She's a different story."

But I didn't get to hear that story. With the next pain Venice grabbed her knees again. Her scrunched face reddened with exertion. I grabbed the top couple of cloths off the stack and spread one under her buttocks. I drew the cord scissors out of my satchel even as a tiny dark-haired head appeared at the opening. Such an early baby was likely to be small and present little difficulty in birthing. Whether its lungs would be mature enough to sustain life was a different question.

A blessed hour later the swaddled babe was in his mother's arms, with his grandfather in a chair at the bedside. The birth had been as easy as they come. Venice's passageway had not torn, the afterbirth had been intact, the little fellow had breathed well, and he'd already suckled his first meal. He now regarded Venice with the calm dark-eyed gaze of all newborns.

Venice glanced at her father. "*Papere*, I was going to name him Joseph. But now I must call him Warren. You understand, *n'est ce pas*?"

He nodded, tears again in his eyes.

"I have something I must do," I said, patting my pocket. "I'll return before nightfall to check on thee, Venice. And I'll bring an herb to help thy milk production."

"You're a *traiteur*, Rose. What we call a healer back home." Venice smiled, just a little.

I smiled back.

***

I hurried along the lower edge of Main Street back to the river, the mid-afternoon sun glinting off the water. After I chatted with several neighbors of the steamboat office, as well as with a man running a fish shop next door to the dock, I hailed the horse-drawn trolley that ran from the bridge into town. I'd put together two and two and I urgently needed to convey the sum to a certain detective. But first I had a bit of research to do.

Twenty minutes after alighting downtown, I laid out my idea to Kevin in his office.

"This is quite a stretch, Miss Rose."

"I believe thee holds an innocent man, Kevin. Doesn't thee wish to see justice served?"

He stared at me, finally letting out a long sigh. "All right. I'll check that one fact, and then let's be off."

Half an hour later we stood in the clean but somewhat shabby parlor of the Daigle home, a small house near the rail depot. Addie again wore the pink and red-sprigged day dress I'd seen her in yesterday.

"What do you want?" she asked. "You already have my husband."

Kevin nodded to me.

"Thee knows thy husband is suspected of killing Warren Currier this morning."

She kneaded one hand with the other. "I was just on my way to the jail to visit him. My poor Anton was under such pressure."

"What kind of pressure?" Kevin asked, pulling out a small notebook and a stub of pencil.

"Working the two businesses up here. He'd escaped the Ring down there in New Orleans where he's from. But the work was just about killing him. I'm not surprised he cracked."

"Did he?" I asked. "Where was thee this morning a few minutes before dawn?"

"Asleep here in my bed, of course."

I gave a brief nod to Kevin, who went into the hall and returned with Addie's fanciful red hat.

"Sure enough, it's from Mrs. Hallowell's," he said after examining the tag inside.

"What d'you want with my hat?" Addie tried to grab it but Kevin was too fast for her.

I pulled out the feather from my pocket and held it up next to the three small white feathers that were part of the hat's decoration.

"A perfect match," I said. "Mrs. Hallowell herself told me these are most rare, feathers from a nearly extinct African miniature heron. She had only the four."

"And what of it?" Addie scoffed. "I've gone into the steamship office many times wearing that hat."

I glanced at Kevin. I hadn't said the office was where I'd found the feather.

Kevin drew out a handkerchief and carefully extracted a long hat pin from the bow at the back of the hat, a pin with rust-colored stains. "I daresay our microscope will discover traces of Mr. Currier's blood on your hat pin, ma'am."

"And I believe we'll find spots of blood mixing in with the red flowers on thy dress," I added. "A neighbor saw thee enter the office early this morning. Thy own husband said thee was not in the marital bed when he arose." I wondered how she knew how to find the carotid, but perhaps it had been luck, not skill.

Addie turned to look out the window.

"Why did you kill him, Mrs. Daigle?" Kevin stood tall, official, stern.

She faced us, head held high. "I deserve a better life than this. We never have enough money." With a curled lip she gestured around the room. "I didn't think Anton would be stupid enough to get himself arrested. I thought we'd get the whole business for ourselves."

"Thee seemed willing to let us think Anton was the murderer a moment ago."

"Well, *I* certainly didn't want to be hauled off to jail." She tossed her blond curls. "And if he's guilty, then the business is mine, isn't it?"

"I guess you never read their business contract," Kevin said in a soft voice. "In case of one partner's death, his half of the enterprise goes to his wife."

"No!" Her eyes went wide. She lunged for Kevin, her fingernails aiming for his neck. Kevin neatly sidestepped and caught her hands behind her. He gave a whistle, and another officer hurried in from the hall to cuff Addie's hands behind her back. He turned her toward the door.

She twisted back to glare at Kevin and me. "You'll regret this."

"I doubt it," he murmured.

***

I approached the Currier home as dusk fell to find Joseph and Anton leaving the house. I supposed Anton might be angry with me for my role in Addie's arrest, but I greeted them, regardless.

"How is Venice?" I asked. "I brought her the herb I'd promised."

"She is grieving terribly," Joseph said. "But at least she has her baby." He clapped a hand on Anton's shoulder. "And we're putting up my nephew for the time being."

"It's generous of you, *Nonc* Joseph." He looked at me. "I have to sell my house now, to pay for my wife's lawyer."

"I see," I said. "Perhaps you heard of the assistance I provided the detective. I'm sorry--"

Anton held up a hand. "Addie did a terrible thing, and you made sure justice was served. Please don't apologize." His face sagged but he kept his chin up and shoulders back.

I nodded in silence.

"We're off to church to say a prayer for both Warren and his baby son." Joseph tipped his hat.

The two climbed into the waiting carriage. I knocked at the house, relieved to leave detecting behind. I had a new mother and baby to see to.

Adam and Eva

Author Note: I wrote this story from Bertie Winslow's point of view. She often helps Rose solve cases and I wanted to give the petite post-master one of her own.

Who wouldn't be smitten with Adam Osgood?

My young assistant, Eva Stillwell, stood behind the counter of the Amesbury Post Office where I, Bertie Winslow, serve as Postmistress. I watched as Eva handed Adam his stamps, her eyes aglow. President Grover Cleveland also watched from his portrait on the wall. Dark-haired Adam returned Eva's light-eyed gaze with a smile like a sunny idyll. Even their names were a match made in Eden.

I doubted this dalliance would come right in the end, though. Eva's family belonged to the Religious Society of Friends. Adam's was Episcopalian. Eva's father worked at Osgood Carriage Manufacturers. Adam's father owned the factory. Still, Adam was a gentle young man. He had an open, kind manner about him, and he adored Eva.

"Eva," I said without harshness. "You've customers waiting." Two gentlemen and a young lady formed a line at Eva's window in air that smelled comfortingly of ink, polished wood, and mucilage.

"I'm sorry, Miss Winslow," she answered softly.

While I sat at my desk and managed the administration of the postal system, Eva was my sole office employee. She sold stamps, calculated postage due on packages, and did every other task for our bustling town's postal service, save making the twice-daily delivery rounds to businesses and residences. For that I had a crew of hardy men who ventured forth even in snow, sleet, and blazing heat.

Adam leaned over and whispered to Eva, bringing a blush up to the roots of her auburn hair. I'd known curly-haired Adam since he was a boy. I'd known Eva almost as long through my midwife friend Rose Carroll, also a Quaker, and I was fond of both young people.

Adam touched his bowler and turned to go. He hadn't made it to the outer door when the tall young lady in line touched his arm. About Adam's age, she sported a pink and black ensemble with the new slim silhouette.

"Oh, Mr. Osgood." A fancy hat in the latest fashion, trimmed with feathers to match her dress, sat at a gravity-defying angle.

"Miss Hamilton." Adam tipped his hat and took a step toward the door.

This was Lily Hamilton, the middle daughter of the town's most prosperous mill owner, if I wasn't mistaken.

"Do stay and keep me company, will you?" She batted dark lashes. "I'm so unaccustomed to be out and about doing business."

Adam smiled politely to Lily and nodded. "How've you been faring?"

"I just returned from finishing school in Switzerland, where I won several prizes for my equestrian abilities. Don't I recall you have a fondness for horses, yourself?"

I glanced at Eva in her somber green dress, free of lace or flounce. Even the buttons were plain, covered in the fabric of the dress. The cut of the garment more or less matched Lily's, but without any of the fancy touches. While Eva handed a parcel to the next customer in line, her troubled glance flitted to Adam and Lily.

"Why, yes, I do." Adam let out a breath and checked his pocket watch. "Dear me, look at the time. If you'll excuse me, Miss

Hamilton, I have an appointment."

"Do come riding with me, Mr. Osgood. I want to get to know you better." She regarded him with cocked head.

Adam touched his hat again and hurried out. Lily was the next customer at the counter.

"I'm waiting for a package. For Miss Lily Hamilton." Lily didn't meet Eva's gaze nor say "if you please."

"Please wait." Eva turned away and searched the bins at the back of the office, one by one. On her way back to the counter, she glanced at me. "I can't locate it," she whispered.

I shrugged. "Likely still in the post."

"I'm sorry. Thy parcel hasn't yet arrived," Eva told Lily.

"Are you sure? Look again, girl." Lily waved her hand.

"Thy parcel hasn't yet arrived." Eva stood tall. "Thee may ask again tomorrow."

"What are you, one of those Quakers?" Lily scoffed. "With your thees and thys." She turned to go, muttering, "Lunatics are everywhere these days."

***

Rose and I strolled up to the five-story red brick Opera House that evening, with its slate roof slanting down to meet tile-work depicting the dramatic arts. I'd invited Rose to attend a performance of Strindberg's play *Miss Julie*, which he'd written just the year before.

Rose, fifteen years my junior and a committed Friend, wore her best cloak over her best deep red dress, all without other adornment, of course. I'd indulged in a new hat for the occasion, since hair ornamentation was my great weakness.

"Isn't it splendid?" I glanced up at my taller friend as we gained entrance to the foyer. Glass chandeliers sparkled with gas flames, and rich velvet hangings decorated the walls. A cluster of young people stood near the double doors that opened onto the theater itself. I spied a clutch of youthful dandies, including

Adam Osgood and Tobias Clark, talking with Lily Hamilton and several other young ladies in their evening finery. Eva was not among them.

As we approached, Lily attached herself to Adam's arm and gazed up at him. A wan smile overtook his face, matched by a furrowed brow. When we passed by, he cleared his throat and detached himself. Lily's nostrils flared as she glared at us.

"Good evening, Miss Carroll, Miss Winslow." Now Adam's smile was genuine, the beam of light I was accustomed to seeing in his open face.

"Hello, Adam. How is thee?" Rose asked.

"I'm well, thank you. I look forward to tonight's entertainment." He took a step away from the group.

"As do we," I said, handing our tickets to the gentleman at the door.

"A pleasure to see you both." Adam bowed.

We started to follow the usher to our seats. At the sound of raised voices, I halted and glanced back. Rose turned, too. Silhouetted by the bright lights in the foyer, Tobias Clark grasped Adam by the collar.

"How dare you consort with my Lily?" the fellow shouted. "She is betrothed to me."

"I...I did nothing, Tobias," Adam protested. He held up both hands.

Lily pushed her way between them. "Tobias, drop your silly notion of betrothal. Our parents thought it would be amusing if we married, but that was arranged before I went away to school. Everything's different now."

Even from several yards distant, I could see the fury on Tobias's face. He turned and stalked away.

***

I clattered down Main Street two days later at nearly five in the morning on my horse, Grover. On the summer solstice I liked to take in the sunrise from the river's vista, early though it was. I soon reached the wide Merrimack and dismounted near the Morrill coal wharf, inhaling the fresh scent of flowing water. An eagle snagged a wriggling fish in its powerful talons and beat strong wings to land on a high branch.

I was tying Grover's reins to a hitching post when a woman approached on a safety bicycle, cloak flying behind her, bonnet hanging by its strings down her back.

"Rose Carroll, is that you?" I waved.

"It is I." When she drew close, she came to a stop, setting one foot on the ground, I saw dark smudges under her eyes. A bulging satchel hung from a handlebar. "And what business has thee down here so early in the morning?"

"I like to watch the sun come up on the longest day of the year. And you, friend? I'd wager you've been helping a new person into the world all night."

She nodded. "Yes, a healthy baby girl, praise God. But the mother labored since yesterday noon. I'll watch the sunrise with thee, then I'm off for my bed. The older Hamilton daughter is due to deliver any day now, as well. My practice is almost busier than I can handle."

She leaned her metal steed against a post. We picked our way through low brush down to the shore. The air was mild but promised heat by midday. I spied a large log that would make a perfect viewing bench.

"Let's sit there." I pointed.

Rose's gaze followed mine, but her eyes widened. She brought a hand to her mouth. "Oh, no." She hurried ahead and made her way around the other side of the log. She gestured urgently for me to follow before kneeling almost out of sight. Had she seen something with her height that I could not? I followed her, then stopped short.

Adam Osgood, arms sprawled wide, eyes on eternity, lay with

the waters of the Merrimack lapping his feet and legs. He was no longer of this world.

Rose gazed up at me. "Poor Adam." Her mouth turned down and her eyes filled.

"Poor Adam, indeed. How in tarnation did he die, and land here, too?" I frowned, and squatted next to him. I felt his jacket, his shirt. "All his clothes are wet, not only his trousers. Do you think he died by drowning?"

She leaned over him. She pushed wide his eyelids and peered at his eyes, then gently stroked both lids closed. After she sniffed at his nose and mouth, she lifted his head and examined the back.

"I see no wound. His skin doesn't appear to have been immersed in the water for long. There's no blood nor any bullet holes. But I detect a scent about his mouth that I find curious. Come and smell." She sat back on her heels.

"Must I? I'm not drawn to smelling a dead man, even Adam." I shuddered.

"Well, it's the odor of laudanum."

"Opium in brandy."

"Exactly." Rose nodded. "Although the concoction is properly used to lessen pain, sometimes unhappy wives in higher society take it to avoid the tedium of their lives."

"I wonder why a healthy, content young man would be indulging in such a thing. It surprises me greatly." I stared at him, then looked at Rose. "Think I'd better ride for the police, for your Detective Donovan?" Rose had worked with the able detective on more than one case in the past, and I had assisted her once, myself. In her midwifery practice, she heard secrets from women with child and in travail, women who lived in the richest mansions to the poorest tenements. Secrets that sometimes helped put criminals behind bars.

"Yes. His death could've been accidental." Rose stroked Adam's brow. "But it might have been murder."

***

I rode back to the water, having extracted a promise from Detective Donovan that he would send the wagon down directly. As Grover trotted, I reflected on how distraught Eva would be to lose her sweet beau. As would be Adam's parents. Being financially comfortable was no guarantee against death or any other wrenching loss.

The police wagon passed me near Patten's Hollow. By the time I arrived back at the river, Rose stood near her bicycle. The sun's orb glistened as the broad expanse of water flowed toward the Atlantic. Uniformed officers clustered around Adam's body.

"I thank thee, Bertie," Rose said. "It would've taken me much longer to have cycled all the way into town and back. But thee missed thy sunrise on the river."

"I daresay it'll rise again tomorrow."

Rose's hand could not disguise her yawn. "Forgive me."

"Did Donovan say you needed to stay here?"

She nodded. "He asked me to, because I told him I had a suspicion this was not an accidental death."

A moment later up strode the detective. He regarded both of us, his hands on his robust stomach.

"Now what's this idea you have about young Osgood's death?" His round face was ruddy from his exertions.

"While his clothes were wet," Rose began, "I didn't find any evidence of him hitting his head, and his skin didn't have the look that comes from being immersed in water."

"Very good. I noticed the same," the detective said.

"Did you smell his mouth and nose?" I asked.

He frowned. "No."

Rose told him about detecting laudanum, her face somber. "I don't believe he'd suffered an injury warranting pain-numbing laudanum," she said

"Those rich young folks will do anything to have fun these days," Kevin scoffed.

"He might have been rich, but he was a sober, kind, honest fellow, Kevin." Rose gazed at him. "I believe someone might have dosed him, and then pushed him into the river. I don't know if his body snagged on a limb, or if he crawled up the bank and then died from the dosage." Poor exhausted Rose stood less and less tall by the minute.

"That's your job to figure out, isn't it, Detective?" I asked.

"We'll look into it. Find out who his friends were. See if he had any enemies, young as he was. And so on and so forth. But first I have to notify Mr. and Mrs. Osgood. I don't look forward to that."

***

It was a long and distressing day. In the post office, Eva had gone white at the news, and I'd offered to send her directly back home. She insisted on working, although she did it with reddened eyes and pale cheeks. It had also proved to be a warm day, in fact, and the air in the office grew stultifying even with the small breeze that passed through the windows.

Not a townsperson came in who didn't want to talk about the death with me and with each other. Many remained in the office after they conducted their business. They stood in small clusters speculating that Adam had taken his own life, or that the slippery banks of the river were no place to cavort. Eva seemed to reel at each remark.

When I arrived at my modest cottage at day's end, Rose sat on the bench in my garden, surrounded by a profusion of the flowers I loved to tend. Her cycle leaned against the lamp post.

"What, can't get enough of my lovely face?" I teased her. I tied Grover to the post and sank down next to her, loosening the neck button of my shirtwaist. "Did you find some rest?"

She nodded. "Yes, but not enough. I couldn't stop thinking

about Adam's death. I wanted to talk with thee before I'm off to the Hamilton household. Juliette appears to be in labor, but it's early stages yet."

"The daughter you mentioned?"

"Yes. She is married, of course, but they live across the river, and she wished to have her baby in her parents' home. The girls in that family always get what they want."

"That's how Lily struck me." I reminded Rose about the scene at the Opera House. "She seemed furious that Adam rejected her advances."

"Do you think she would have killed him for that?" she asked.

"Gracious, I certainly hope not." I reached out to pluck a stem of pink sweet pea from the trellis that arched over the path, and smelled deeply of the flower's delicate scent.

A patrol wagon pulled by two horses stopped in front of the house. Detective Donovan jumped down.

"Just the ladies I wanted to see. Came looking for you, Miss Winslow, but having Miss Carroll here, too, is a bonus."

"Kevin, please call me Rose." She gazed at him over the top of her spectacles. Rose must have asked him that a hundred times. She'd told me about how Quakers don't use titles for anyone, following their admirable principle of equality.

"Oh, for land's sake, Miss Ca—Miss Rose. You know that goes against everything my sainted mother drummed into me." He shook his head, but smiled.

Rose smiled back. "What news has thee?"

His mouth turned down. "I've arrested Tobias Clark for the death of Adam Osgood. Thought you might like to know, being as how you found the body."

"You've found evidence linking him to Adam's death, then?" I asked.

"It's more circumstantial, like. Clark and Osgood were together in the tavern last night. Clark claims they parted ways after that, of course. But he's a devious type, and accustomed to having his way. And he's been known to indulge in opium."

Rose and I exchanged a glance. "So thee has no proof?" She narrowed her eyes.

Kevin set his hands on his hips. "The boy has no one to vouch for his whereabouts until after dawn, when you discovered young Osgood."

"Did you ask the residents of the area if anyone was seen near the coal wharf in the hours after Adam was last spotted in public?" I removed my hat and fanned myself with it. The heat had barely abated since its apex in the early afternoon.

"Haven't had anyone come forward to report such a sighting." He tipped his hat. "Ladies, I merely wanted to inform you of the arrest. I didn't expect to be interrogated, myself. Good day."

After he huffed off, I glanced at Rose. "What do you think?"

"It doesn't feel right to me. That solution is too easy."

I nodded. "Exactly."

***

I ate my supper at the small table in the back garden, the shady arbor providing a cooler setting than indoors. A bright yellow warbler flitted in the green leaves of the lilac, and a chipmunk scolded from the branches of the swamp oak overhead.

That Tobias could be arrested without any proof whatsoever nagged at my brain. Perhaps the detective had overlooked a clue of some kind. As the sun neared its evening rest, I mounted Grover again and retraced our steps to the river.

I poked around the bushes near where Rose had found Adam's body. I scanned the rocks that lined the river. I even crept around the edge of the piles of coal on the wharf, but didn't see anything untoward, nothing that didn't belong there. I don't know what I expected. With the sun almost disappearing into the Merrimack, it was time to go.

I untied Grover and hoisted myself over his back, my skirt riding up over the long bloomers of matching cloth I always wore underneath. As I straightened in the saddle, I glimpsed a splash of pink in a tree, and it wasn't a flowering tree. Clucking to Grover, I moved him closer until I could pluck the object from where it was caught on a low branch.

I sat examining it, then secured it in my bosom. If that wasn't the feather from Lily's hat, I would be most surprised. It wasn't proof she killed Adam, of course, but it showed she'd been here, and recently.

***

The next day, I rode the few blocks to Rose's during my mid-day dinner break. She opened the door, pushing her glasses up on her nose, and invited me in.

"I can't tarry but I wanted to show you." I produced the feather. I had penned a quick note to Rose after arriving home last night and had paid a boy to deliver the message to the Hamilton home where she was attending the birth. "I found it right where we discovered poor Adam. I'm sure it's from Lily's hat."

She nodded. "And look what I discovered last night after I assisted in the birth of Juliette's baby boy. Because of thy note, I ventured into Lily's room while she was occupied with the newborn." Rose produced a blue glass vial from her satchel, then uncorked and proffered it. "Smell."

I obliged, then stared at her. "Laudanum. But even these together aren't going to convince Donovan that a slip of a girl killed Adam instead of Tobias Clark. Especially a girl from a prominent family. Many ladies indulge in the drug. And who doesn't wear pink these days?" At her wry smile, I added, "Besides you Quakers, of course."

"She's not a slip of a girl. She's as tall as I. And she told Adam she'd won equestrian prizes. Surely she's strong enough to push an unsuspecting and drugged man into the river."

"We need a plan." Rose frowned.

I nodded, and decided to tarry, after all.

***

After the post office closed at five, I told Eva our idea. After only a moment's hesitation, she agreed. We hurried to my house and hitched Grover to my small carriage that featured a rumble seat in the rear. After we fetched Rose, we headed out to the equestrian ring in West Amesbury.

"Do you think Kevin received thy note?" Rose asked in a soft voice.

"I surely hope so." I pulled up at the far edge of the stable. As we had planned, Rose and I strolled over to the field, leaving Eva with Grover. Observers clustered at a fence surrounding the large oval ring. Inside, several ladies cantered sidesaddle, their small black toppers worn forward on their heads. Despite the cultured look of the scene, the aroma of pungent manure filled my nostrils.

"There she is," Rose said pointing.

Lily, in a royal blue habit, rode with erect back atop a spirited black beast. After she dismounted and handed the reins to a boy, we waylaid her before she reached the refreshments tent.

"Miss Hamilton," I said. "Lovely riding."

"Thank you, Miss Winslow. Oh, hello, Rose." Lily's cheeks were bright from her exercise in the still-warm evening.

"I wondered if you'd take a look at my own steed, tell me if he has potential for competing," I said.

Lily narrowed her eyes. "You want to enter an equestrian competition?"

"I was thinking about it. Grover is just over here." I led the way. Eva was out of sight.

"This old gelding?" Lily made a *tsking* sound when we stood at Grover's side. "You need a better horse than that to compete. My Blackie is a hot-blood thoroughbred."

"Oh, well. Say, I rode Grover down to the river last night. I found one of your pink feathers in a tree there." I watched her. Rose did, too.

Lily blinked several times. "My pink feather? Surely you jest." She spoke fast, and didn't meet my gaze.

"And I found this in your room after your nephew was born." Rose drew the laudanum bottle out of a small cloth bag.

Lily extended her hand to snatch it, but Rose pulled it back. "We know thee drugged Adam Osgood and then pushed him into the river."

"I did no such thing," she exclaimed, glancing from Rose to me and back. "Why would I? I was fond of Adam. I wanted him to court me."

"Because he scorned you, more than once, that's why," I said. "He was in love with Eva Stillwell, and she with him."

"That mousy little thing?" Her lip curled. "What could he have seen in her?"

"Me?" Eva strolled around the side of the stable, hands clasped in front of her.

"You!" Lily's pretty mouth turned down in a nasty expression.

Eva kept her voice level. "Adam loved me, you know."

"He had it coming to him, rejecting me for you. It was all his fault." She looked with scorn at Rose, then at me. "My father has great influence in this town. I'll have him publicly chastise you three for even suggesting I killed Adam."

"How did you get out at night alone?" I asked.

"I do what I wish." She raised her chin. "I slipped out of the house in a dark cloak and rode Blackie. Tobias told me the boys were going to bathe in Lake Gardner after they went drinking. I promised Adam he could ride Blackie if he'd come with me, instead."

"How did thee drug him?" Rose folded her arms.

"I told him I'd brought cognac from Paris and offered it to

him in that bottle. He was already half gone from what he'd imbibed with Tobias, so he didn't taste the opium." She sniffed. "I never would've done it if he hadn't shunned me. Now, if you'll excuse me, I'm here to ride."

"Not so fast, young lady." Detective Donovan also stepped out from around the corner of the stable. "Miss Lily Hamilton, you are under arrest for the murder of Adam Osgood." He strode toward her and grasped her hand.

"I didn't kill Adam! Take your hands off me, you filthy copper."

"I heard every word you just said to these ladies." Donovan slid a handcuff around Lily's wrist and clicked it into place. As he reached for her other hand, she slapped him across the face and twisted away, but she was no match for Amesbury's finest. I'd never heard such a satisfying sound as the *snick-snick* of the second handcuff securing Lily's hands behind her back.

She glowered at us before Donovan marched her away. "You tricked me. Father will make you pay for this."

I raised my eyebrows at Rose and Eva. "How about if this old presidential gelding takes us home?" I stroked Grover's neck.

Rose nodded. "Lily wanted to be the apple of Adam's eye."

Eva watched Donovan load Lily into the wagon. "She ended up the snake in the garden."

A Fire in Carriagetown

Author Note: This story kicked off the entire Quaker Midwife series. It's told from Rose's niece Faith Bailey's point of view, and astute readers will notice Rose Carroll isn't even in it. After I moved to Amesbury in 2012 and read about the Great Fire of 1888, this story came to me. It was published, but the era and the setting refused to vacate my brain. I thought an adult protagonist would work better in a novel, so Rose Carroll was born, as was *Delivering the Truth*, the first book of seven, first published in 2016.

I lifted my skirts and stepped over a pile of manure at the edge of High Street, then dropped them quickly before anyone could glimpse my boot-clad ankles. I dipped my head under my plain bonnet as I passed Father Nilan climbing into a carriage.

Mother had instructed me to keep my head up when I encountered any adult, whether the priest of Saint Joseph's or President Cleveland. As members of the Society of Friends, she told me, we believe in equality under God. That was why my father did not doff his simple hat when he met an Amesbury selectman on the street and why we did not use titles to address each other, not even children to adults.

But Mother was dead. My best friend at Hamilton Mills, Annie Beaumont, respected her priest. I didn't want to tempt fate by not showing him conventional courtesy.

I hurried past the closing shops on Market Street. A bitter wind rushed up from the Powow River despite it being past the spring equinox. The thrum of the textile mills' water wheels filled my ears. I pulled my shawl closer around my neck as I trudged up Carriage Hill, hoping to catch my fellow, Zebulon, when he finished his shift. Zeb worked longer hours than I, and I pined to see him as he exited Babcock's Carriage Factory. In rushing, my ankle turned on a cobblestone. An arm reached out to break my fall.

"In such a hurry to see my brother, Faith?"

I straightened and smiled at my tall rescuer. "I thank thee, Isaiah. I admit to an eagerness that overruled caution." I surveyed the road outside the factory gates. Workers trickled out from the ironwork opening, but it wasn't the usual surge. "Is Zeb working late?"

"He wasn't scheduled to work longer than his twelve hours." Isaiah frowned. "But we are on different shifts. Mine starts now and continues until dawn."

"I am fortunate to work only ten-hour shifts." Twelve would do me in. Since Mother died and I had taken her job at the mill, I felt a tiredness that barely went away by the end of First Day. My feet hurt constantly and my ears rang after a day monitoring four of the hundred looms in a room so noisy from the machinery one could not converse. But I was the eldest, seventeen and strong. Father, a teacher at the Academy, couldn't take on the burden of five children alone, no matter how much we both wanted me to continue my education.

"Did thee see my Annie this day?" he asked.

"Only on our break. It must be hard for thee to find time for each other, working opposite shifts."

He smiled ruefully. "Indeed. 'Tis only on Saturday and First Day we can visit."

A man in a ragged cap pushed by us on his way out. Isaiah reached out an arm to steady me.

"Ephraim Pickard!" Isaiah called. "Has thee changed thy work to the day shift?"

The man turned, glowering. "They've given me the boot. I was on warning. And now how will I feed the family, what barely gets enough as it is?" The collar of his woolen coat shone from years of wear and a neatly sewn patch at the shoulder was beginning to fray.

"Why did they release thee?" Isaiah asked.

"That son of Mr. Babcock's said I was late once too often." He shook his head, a fiery look on his face. "And he didn't like me reading on my lunch break. How's a man supposed to get ahead?" He clomped away with uneven gait, a tattered book in one hand.

"More's the pity. Thomas Babcock isn't much of a manager." Isaiah watched Ephraim go. "I'd best go in so I don't risk being late myself." He smiled. "I'm sure Zebulon will appear in a moment."

I bade him farewell as he strode toward the two-story wooden factory. I waited, pacing outside the tall fence, inhaling the sharp smell of impending rain. I squinted at the large clock on the building's face. I must have missed Zeb. I'd tarried too long putting supper on the stove at home. When the lamplighter came along, I knew I had to make my way back without seeing my suitor.

The damp wind chilled me as I began to descend Carriage Hill. I whirled when I spied a moving shape in the gloaming. I peered back at the side of the carriage factory. Someone was creeping by the fence, seemingly with a limp. The shape dissolved into the falling darkness. I shuddered and shook my head before I continued on my way.

***

Several hours later I sat by the fire with Father and Luke. Father read while Luke, thirteen, did ciphers for school. The twins, Matthew and Mark, and eight-year old Betsy slept upstairs in our tidy home a short way up the hill from the mill where I worked.

The mill owner, George Farley, had ordered the dwelling built to house his workers while Mother was still alive. Normally it would have been let out to a male employee. But Father had given special tutoring to George Farley's difficult son. The owner apparently felt he owed Father some kind of debt. When Mother died and the first occupants left town, George Farley offered us the house.

I had been darning but I must have fallen asleep. When bells began clanging in town my eyes flew open.

"It's the fire bell." Father was on his feet. He pushed up the sash and sniffed. "I smell smoke."

Luke darted upstairs. A moment later he was back.

"It's on Carriage Hill. The flames are shooting into the sky!"

"I hope it's not the Babcock factory. Isaiah is at work." I brought my hand to my mouth. I smelled fire, too.

The three of us rushed up the stairs, then tiptoed into the bedroom Luke shared with the sleeping twins. We clustered around the windows and opened one to the cold air. Flames teased ever higher into the black sky and the smell of smoke snapped at my nose. I couldn't tell which of the carriage factories was burning.

The two young men who lived up the road rushed by below, buckets in hand.

"Father, we must go and help." Luke, not yet full-grown and still a stringbean, pulled at Father's sleeve.

"Thee is too young, Luke," Father answered, "and I must stay at home, as well. Amesbury has a fire department and many dedicated volunteers. They will extinguish the fire."

Father stretched an arm around me and laid his other hand on Luke's head. I leaned against his bony shoulder and closed my eyes, holding Isaiah in the Light as a windswept rain dampened our clothing.

***

"How will I live?" wailed Annie.

I embraced her shaking shoulders late the next morning. Indeed, her sweetheart Isaiah had been lost in the fire, along with a dozen other men. I was almost equally sad at losing my tall friend.

The disastrous fire had jumped from Babcock's to the post office and thence to the telegraph office. By the time help arrived from surrounding Haverhill, Lawrence, and Newburyport, the fire had raged all night. It destroyed most of the carriage industry as well as a number of shops and houses, leaving scores of families homeless. Our neighbors had shared the news as they trudged home sooty and exhausted a few hours earlier. Only the rain prevented further damage. I was grateful Zeb had been safe at home, but my heart was heavy from the death of Isaiah and the others.

We sat in Annie's three-room tenement apartment down on the Flats where she lived with her mother, two brothers, and her mother's parents, all French-Canadian, all textile mill workers except her dotty *Grandmère*. Because it was Good Friday, Hamilton Mills was closed. Thankfully it had been spared from the fire, as had the other mills on the Powow.

I stroked Annie's hair. "Thee will live, my friend. Life goes on, no matter how painful." I tucked an errant red curl back under the green ribbon holding it.

She paused her sobbing and gazed into my eyes. "I'm sorry, Faith. Of course you know this better than anyone."

I patted her hand and wondered why God bestowed such hardship upon us. "Thee will come to Isaiah's Memorial Meeting for Worship tomorrow?"

She nodded, her eyes filling again.

I smiled at her. "Thee and thy pretty ribbons. I wish I could wear some."

She smiled wanly. "You should. I'll lend you some."

"No, I have told thee before. Friends are to wear plain dress." I sighed, sweeping my hand over my very plain gray dress. I loved bright colors. "I shall simply enjoy thine."

She pulled the ribbon from her hair and handed it to me. "Take this. Curl it up in your pocket. Wear it to bed. Do with it what you'd like, even if it is only gazing upon it."

"Thank thee, Annie. Now I must get home." I squeezed her hand. "Be well, friend."

***

I walked slowly back up Water Street to Market Square. Wet ash coated awnings and smelled of sadness. The storm had blown through leaving a sunny, breezy day at odds with the town's mood. Residents and businesspeople talked outside in small clumps with much shaking of heads and faces red with anger at the town's failure to extinguish the fire. Amesbury's graceful well-built carriages were famous nationwide. I overheard an older man refer to it as the Great Fire of 1888.

Several men standing outside Sawyer's Mercantile included Stephen Farley, the student Father had taught and tried to help. Now in his twenties, he wore a coat of fine cloth and carried a Bible in his hand, but his hat sat askew. Mud covered his fancy boots. He shook the book in their faces.

"Now settle down, Farley. Everything is God's will. Even accidents," an older man said.

Stephen wagged his head and pointed a trembling finger. His eyes burned with anger.

"Why don't you go home and try to calm down?"

Stephen Farley stalked away, muttering. As I passed, the other man said, "That boy is touched in the head. He rarely speaks."

"He's no longer a boy," the older man replied. "His father should make him work. He needs a good honest job."

I watched Stephen go, wondering if anyone in his life cared

about him. I made my way up High Street and turned onto the path leading to home.

"Faith!"

I turned to see Zeb hurrying toward me. "Zeb." I held out my hand.

He grasped it in both of his. His usually delighted expression was replaced by haunted eyes and a mouth turned down in grief.

"I am so sorry about dear Isaiah," I murmured. "How is thee? And thy parents?"

"We can barely believe it. And they are saying it might not have been an accident."

"Does thee mean someone set the fire with intent? But who?" A cold knot grabbed my stomach.

"I do not know." He squeezed my hand. "Thee will come to the Memorial Meeting for Worship tomorrow morning?"

"Of course. Annie will attend, too. And I shall bake some sweets for afterwards."

"I must get back to my family. Faith, if only we could roll the clock back to yesterday."

I reached up a hand to stroke his cheek. "If only."

***

I spent the rest of the day doing the washing, scrubbing the kitchen, putting dinner together, and baking dozens of gingersnaps and sugar cookies for the service. The twins and Betsy helped on the last, especially when it came time to clean the remnants of sweet batter from the bowl.

As I worked I mourned for Isaiah. And I thought of all the families now without homes. All the men, mostly, now without jobs. The parents without children and children without parents. Zeb's remark about the fire being set stuck in my brain like the incessant grumble of a mill wheel. That shadowy shape I had seen as I left Babcock's the evening before. Could it have been the arsonist?

My thoughts turned to Ephraim, forced out of his job before the fire. Perhaps he had wanted to destroy the factory that deprived him of his livelihood. When I was finished baking, I packed a basket with a bowl of stew, a loaf of bread, and a small paper of cookies.

"Father, I'm going to pay a visit on the Pickard family. I shall be back for supper," I called into his study.

"Thee is a kind young woman," he called back.

Kind, perhaps. Curious, certainly.

***

The Pickards lived on Friend Street beyond the Meetinghouse in a building housing four families. Ephraim sat on the stoop in the sunlight, a book open on his knees. He looked up when he saw me. He stood, closing the book. His coat fell open, showing a dark smudge on the front of his white shirt.

"Miss Bailey, isn't it?"

"Yes. I brought thy family a meal, Ephraim." I extended the basket.

"We don't need charity." He frowned.

The door opened behind him and two girls about Betsy's age ran out, leaving the door open. One bumped into Ephraim. "Sorry, Papa!" She ran off with a laugh.

"Will thee consider it a gift from a friend instead of charity?"

He nodded slowly.

"Has thee heard talk about the fire, Ephraim?"

"Is there any other talk in town?" He shoved his hands in his pockets and looked away. "It must have been a lazy lamplighter or sparks escaping from the warming stove."

"I have heard it was set with intent."

"Arson." He snapped his head toward me.

I nodded.

"Who would do such a thing?" he asked.

"Who knows? Perhaps someone with a grudge against the

management." The smudge on his shirt looked much like soot.

Scowling, Ephraim stepped toward me. "What do you imply?" he shouted, his fists clenched.

Father often reminded me I needed to temper my natural forthrightness with tact, and I wondered if I had overstepped the bounds.

His daughters ran giggling around the corner of the house. He scooped up one in his arms, still frowning at me. As the girl squealed, a woman with a fat-cheeked baby on one hip appeared in the doorway behind him. The lines in her face measured years of toil and childbearing. She laid a reddened hand on Ephraim's shoulder and squeezed.

"Calm yourself, husband."

Ephraim took a deep breath. "Miss Bailey has kindly brought us a gift of food." He grabbed the basket from my hand and handed it to his wife.

"We gladly accept and thank you, miss."

"There are some sweeties for the children, too," I said, keeping my voice friendly.

A quiet smile spread across her face. "You are very kind. They have few treats." As the baby began to fuss she stepped back into the house and closed the door.

I took my leave. As I glanced back, Ephraim glared at me over his daughter's dark curls.

***

The end of Isaiah's Memorial Meeting drew near. The worship room overflowed with Friends, townspeople, and Isaiah's family and friends.

When I'd entered an hour before, I glanced at Friend John Whittier, already seated with straight back in his customary place. He winked at me, then closed his eyes. I had known the famous poet and abolitionist my entire life. To the outside world he presented a serious, almost stern demeanor. In my experience, he loved young people and was not above a wink to us.

As Clerk of Meeting he had broken the initial silence with a welcome and introduction to worship after the manner of Friends, inviting those present to celebrate the life of Isaiah, whose spirit had been released to God. He asked attenders to leave a few moments of silence between each message. I sensed several non-Quakers' unease with the stillness. For me it provided a lifelong calming comfort.

Stephen Farley arrived late, book in hand, and squeezed into a back-row pew. I didn't know he was a friend of Isaiah's, but it was a public service, after all. He jittered in his seat and never seemed to settle into the quiet place that is Friends' worship. John Whittier, sitting in his usual seat at the end of the facing bench, opened his eyes and trained them on Stephen in a moment of unspoken admonishment.

During the service Annie bravely stood and shared a memory of Isaiah's warmth and humor as they had walked along the Powow one afternoon only a week earlier. After she sat, I held her hand as she wept softly into her kerchief. Seated across the rectangle of pews with his parents and younger siblings, Zeb had waited until nearly the end of Meeting to talk about his brother. When he was finished, he sank back onto the bench and bent over with face in hands, shoulders heaving.

Afterward mourners flowed out onto the grassy area. Several older ladies and I laid out refreshments on a trestle table. The gathering continued on a somber note, with townspeople and friends of Isaiah's offering their condolences to his parents. A knot of young men gathered around Zeb and told stories about escapades with the brothers when they were younger, bringing a much-needed smile to Zeb's face. Stephen Farley stood alone on the periphery of the gathering, his eyes darting here and there.

Kevin Donovan, a police detective I had once met, approached the food table and helped himself to a gingersnap. The ruddy-faced man wore a dark suit instead of a uniform. Perhaps he was a friend of the family. I wondered if I should tell him about the person I had spied near the factory.

"Good morning, Miss Bailey."

"It's a sad day, Detective." I took a breath. "How is the fire investigation going? Has thee found a cause for it?"

He looked sharply toward me. "What business is that of a girl like you?"

"I live in this town." I folded my arms. "My dear friend died in the awful conflagration. And I heard talk yesterday of someone deliberately setting the fire."

"We still seek answers."

"I have some information. Before the fire began I was near Babcock's. And I saw someone outside the fence creeping in stealth, possibly limping. He held an object."

"He?" The detective leaned toward me across the table.

I was startled. "I don't believe the person was wearing skirts. In truth, as it was darkening, I did not see so clearly. It's possible it was a woman."

"And what was the object?"

"It was flat and thick. I could not see more."

"If you remember or think of any other detail, let me know."

I nodded before he turned away, his head moving to scan the assemblage. Perhaps he was not here as a mourner. I surveyed the table and combined two half-full plates of sweets into one. The punch was running scant, so I made my way around the back of the Meetinghouse where we had left an additional jug in the shade of the roof overhang. My feet rustled dry leaves from last autumn. I had hefted the heavy container when Stephen rushed around the far corner. When he spied me he halted.

"Stephen Farley," I called. "We are happy thee could join us."

He strode in my direction. "You Quakers should be quaking

at the wrath of the Lord." Scowling, he shook his Bible in the air.

I held up my hand, relieved he stopped three feet distant and surprised he was speaking. "Our God is a loving one and is in each person. Now, would thee carry this weighty jug for me?" I held out the container.

He blinked several times. The scowl disappeared, replaced by a cautious look. "You want my help?"

I nodded. "If thee please."

He did look pleased. He handed me the book with scarred hands and hefted the jug. I followed him to the front.

"May I help you with anything else, miss?"

He seemed a different person from the wild ranter of a few moments earlier. Perhaps, as the man in town had suggested, Stephen did need a job, or at least an avenue to help others.

"Does thee know aught about who set the fire?" I thought it wouldn't hurt to ask.

He shook his head and strolled away, swinging the Bible.

***

As I prepared the porridge the next morning, my heart continued heavy about Isaiah's loss. I was not paying close attention as I struck a match to light the stove and a spark flew onto my hand. I flicked it onto the stove but my hand stung from the burn. I left the house an hour early, telling Father I would walk to First Day Meeting with Zeb. I made my way to his family's home on Orchard Street. He was surprised to see me, but agreed to my plan.

He tucked my arm through his solid one as we walked toward Carriage Hill. I wanted to see the ruins of the fire. Perhaps if I stood in the same place as before, I might remember more about the figure I had seen and I could report it to Kevin Donovan.

"Zeb, does thee know Stephen Farley?"

He nodded, rolling his eyes. "He's a bit crazy."

"It might do him good to have employment. Why doesn't his father hire him at the mill?"

We arrived at the Babcock manufactory. The wrought iron gates still stood, but the property was now a wasteland of dark shapes. A twisted metal rod stuck up out of a pile of charred timber and the skeleton of a bent wheel lay in a heap of burned parts.

Zeb surveyed the ruins. "I hope my brother did not suffer." His voice quavered.

I stroked his arm as I gazed to the right to where I had seen the figure, but in the cool daylight it didn't even look like the same location.

Zeb took a deep breath. "I heard good news last night. Robert Clarke has decided to rebuild his carriage factory immediately. My father said that might encourage the other owners to do the same, including Babcock."

"Wonderful news."

"Has thee remembered anything else from that night?"

I shook my head. We headed back down the hill toward the Meetinghouse.

"Stephen Farley did work for some time," Zeb said. "On my shift at Babcock's. Thomas Babcock let him go, though. Farley spent every lunch period reading that Bible and exhorting the rest of us to mend our ways. I was glad to see him gone."

A carriage carrying a family clattered by us. The women and girls sported lovely Easter bonnets in spring-like colors. The Society of Friends recognized the sacredness of Easter but did not celebrate with a change in clothing or any special ritual. I secretly longed for a pretty bonnet trimmed in pink and purple like the young women's in the carriage. Instead I fingered Annie's green ribbon in my pocket.

We arrived at Meeting on time. I struggled, as often happened, to tame my thoughts as I sat in worship. The rustling of skirts and adjusting of coats soon quieted until all I heard was the echo of fourscore Friends silently seeking God. I knew I needed to quiet my mind so I could listen for the Light instead of to my own brain. Instead the silence amplified my turmoil.

Agitated, I stared at my hands as I examined my memory as to who might have set the fire. Truly, I had noticed neither trousers nor skirts on the figure in the shadows. Could a woman with a grudge against Mr. Babcock have lit the match? If so, I could not imagine who. Maybe it was crazy Stephen who did the deed. Who knew what thoughts arose in his disturbed mind? I hoped angry Ephraim wasn't the culprit, with those spirited children and his hard-working wife, yet the soot on his shirt could have come from the factory fire.

Suddenly I knew who the firebug was. I had to tell Detective Donovan. I risked disapprobation by leaving Meeting early. Censure was worth it. I rose and made my way to the door. Father opened his eyes and frowned at me but I continued, wincing as I broke the silence by catching my boot toe on the edge of a bench and nearly tripping.

When I closed the outer door behind me, I took a deep breath. I sniffed. It was not the smoke of coal and wood with which every resident in town cooked and heated. The smell brought to mind autumn and crisp apples. I shrugged, setting off for the street. As I passed the corner of the building, I bumped into Stephen Farley. I looked at him with alarm.

"What is thee—" I began.

He spun, running to the back of the Meetinghouse. I picked up my skirts and followed at a trot. He disappeared. When I turned the corner, I halted.

Fire flared up from a pile of burning leaves. It licked at the back wall of the building. Stephen stood watching it with an intense stare, rubbing his hands.

I rushed to the pile. I stamped at it, but it had already begun to eat at the wood above.

"Fire!" I yelled. "Help me, Stephen."

He cackled as the flames crept higher.

I grabbed the Bible from his hand and threw it hard at the high window above us, but it bounced off. It fell on the flames and began to burn. Stephen didn't move.

Desperate, I leaned down and grabbed a stone. This time I aimed at the bottom pane and used all my strength. It shattered the pane.

"Fire! Get out!" I screamed. "Fire! Bring buckets!" I heard a shriek from within.

He turned toward me. "I saw how you looked at me, asking me about the fire." He waved his hands, which were covered with phosphorus marks from the matches he must have been lighting every chance he got. This was what I had realized during worship.

Coughing from the smoke, I threw my cloak onto the burning leaves but the fire was too large to smother. "Thee set the factory aflame." I beat at the burning wall with my hands. I wouldn't let my beloved Meetinghouse fall victim to Stephen's warped mind.

He threw his head back and laughed again. "Thomas Babcock looked at me the same way."

Suddenly we were surrounded by Friends. Stephen tried to slip away but Zeb and another young man wrestled him to the ground. Others filled bucket of water from the pond down the slope and threw them on the wall. Father, John Whittier, and another elder spread coats on top of the burning leaves, finally extinguishing the flames. Someone hailed a passing police officer, who cuffed Stephen's hands behind his back. I explained what Stephen had said. The officer said Detective Donovan would find me and marched the still-grinning arsonist away.

I sank to the ground fearing my shaky legs would no longer hold me. Father knelt by my side.

"My brave girl. What made thee discover poor Stephen and the fire?"

"I saw the marks on his hands yesterday. When I lit the stove this morning, a bit of phosphorus split off and singed my own hand. But it wasn't until my thoughts ranged far from the Light this morning that I realized those marks were a sign of a careless person lighting match after match."

"By breaking the silence thee saved us all and our Meetinghouse." Father squeezed my shoulders.

For this I was grateful. And prayed I would not have occasion to meet an arsonist ever again.

The Case of the Missing Bicycle

Author Note: I heard about a Texas gardening magazine looking for short crime fiction. This story was the result.

After I left a client whose baby I was blessedly able to save in my role as midwife, I cycled to my next pregnant client's home on a warm June Saturday in 1888, my birthing satchel tied to the new metal platform on the back of my bicycle.

Fannie Elwood was a month away from birthing her fifth child. When she opened the door to her flat, she looked nearly ready to pop. Or collapse from exhaustion.

"Come in, Rose." She stood with her palms supporting her lower back and her enormous belly pushed out her worn work dress.

A boy slid past us. His face was clean, but his shirt had been many-times mended and his pants were too short and too tight. Children outgrow their clothing so quickly.

"Ma, I done my chores. I'm going out to earn some pennies bringing water to the baseball players." He tugged a cap onto his head. "I promise I'll bring it all back to you."

"Gabe, say hello to Miss Carroll, now," his mother admonished.

"Hello, ma'am." He touched his cap.

"Hello, Gabe. Thee can call me Rose." I extended my hand.

"You one of them Quakers?" His eyes flew wide but he put his small rough hand in mine with a bit of swagger.

"I am." I smiled as he turned and trotted down the stairs.

"Be back for your supper," Fannie called after him. She gazed at me, deep lines creeping along her forehead. """He's a good boy, but he tries too hard to take the place of our late Mr. Elwood. Gabe's almost nine. He should be able to just be a boy a little while longer."

* * *

At the bottom of Fannie's steps an hour later, I stared. My iron steed was not leaning against the hitching post where I'd left it. I looked up and down busy School Street, hands on my hips, but the bicycle was nowhere to be seen. I depended on that cycle to get to clients in a timely fashion. What wretch had stolen it? I'd just added the rack, too, so I didn't have to ride one-handed balancing my satchel on the front. Grumbling, I headed to the police station to report the theft, but the officer at the desk didn't offer much hope of finding the culprit.

Now I wandered through the riot of color that was my friend Bertie's front garden, a tangle of flowers and greenery in all hues and shapes. I gave a drink from the watering can to several pots of pansies wilting from the heat. Bertie was away in Boston and I'd promised to keep her plants from expiring.

Warm from walking, I made my way to the welcome shade of the back garden, just across the fence in back of Fannie's building, and lounged on a bench under Bertie's enormous elm tree. Fragrant sweet peas clung gracefully to strings trained up the shed wall and smelled like a letter from my childhood.

* * *

The next afternoon I trudged back toward Bertie's after the conclusion of Friends Meeting. I'd held the bicycle thief in the Light of God during silent worship but did not discern what path I could follow to regain my cycle. I supposed a thief might be in greater need of transport than I, but my Christian charity didn't extend quite that far. I wished I'd purchased a Yale & Towne padlock and a chain so I would still have my ride.

I rounded a corner and stopped short. A man furiously pedaled a bicycle past me, bumping along the cobblestones. I stepped back, nearly falling into a hedge, but I kept my gaze on the bike, which featured a rack on the back.

"Hold up there," I shouted, but the man raced away. I hadn't seen any other bikes beside mine fitted out like that but apparently there were. I'd taken a closer look before he escaped. Mine was a ladies model; his featured the horizontal bar between seat and handlebars which strengthened the frame for heavier male riders.

After I pumped water at Bertie's and drank deeply of it, I refilled the watering can. As I pushed aside branches of a tall lilac to water a cascading geranium suspended from a dogwood, I froze. Nestled between the greenery and the back fence was a bicycle. I peered at it and recognized the bright welding where my rack attached to the ladies frame. I was about to wrestle it out of the bushes when I heard a rustling and then a sneeze. I backed up with care and waited, hoping my thudding heart wasn't as loud as it sounded in my ears.

A moment later, young Gabe dropped down over the fence. He'd set his hands on the handlebars when I spoke.

"Had need of a bicycle, did thee?" I stepped around the lilac and collared him.

"I don't know what you'd be talking about." His words were brash but his eyes were wide and his voice quavered.

I gazed at him. "Let's get this bike out and then sit for a chat."

A minute later we sat on the shaded bench, the bike resting against my end of the bench. I handed the boy a metal cup of water.

"Gabe, why did thee take my bicycle?" I folded my hands.

He studied the cup, then drained it. "I'm the man of the house now, see? I have to help my ma." He lifted his boyish chin. "I didn't know it was yours. I thought I could make deliveries and earn some real money to help support Ma and the little ones. And the new baby."

"And thee knew Bertie was away and hid my bike here. I might have a solution for thee. But no more stealing. Promise?"

He nodded solemnly. "I promise."

* * *

Gabe's eyes were round and bright as a shiny new pie pan. We stood in front of his home the next day and I pushed the small-framed bicycle toward him a little. A wide basket hung from the handlebars, which also sported a thumb bell.

"Doesn't thee want to try it?" I smiled.

"Oh, yes, ma'am. But why?" he asked with a note of hope.

"It's yours. My friend's son is too big for it now. She wanted thee to have it." I didn't add that the well-off woman and her husband felt they owed me a debt because I'd rescued their newborn daughter from death.

"I'll take good care of it." He stood and squared his young shoulders. "And Miss Carroll? You ever need a delivery, you send for me."

"I'll do that, Gabe." We each would have our own types of deliveries. His, various goods. Mine, babies. As it should be.

A Questionable Death

Author Note: I was delighted this story of Rose and Bertie working together was nominated for a 2015 Agatha Award for Best Short Story.

Helen and I sat on a cloth under a maple tree by the banks of Lake Gardner, the tree's wide leaf-lined branches providing welcome respite from the July midday heat. I loosened the collar of my shirtwaist and fanned myself with my book, one of A.M. Barnard's romantic tales, which I had only recently learned were actually penned by Miss Alcott herself.

"Bertie should be along soon with our picnic," I said.

Helen lay back on the cloth, one arm across her eyes, her pregnant belly pushing her dress up.

"Another dizzy spell?" I asked my client, who was also becoming a friend.

"Yes. They plague me. And my head aches, as well."

"Thy pregnancy is going along normally, though," I reassured her. "And thy baby's heartbeat is strong."

"I suppose you should know, being my midwife." She leaned her head toward me and gave me a faint smile. "Will this all pass once the baby is born?"

"I hope so. Thee has two months to go." In truth I wasn't certain if her symptoms would go away. I wanted my doctor friend David Dodge to examine Helen, but her ill-tempered husband Rupert would not agree.

"Tell me again why you use that old-fashioned manner of speech, with your thees and thys," Helen said.

I laughed. "In earlier times people used *thee* for familiars, and *you* to address those of a higher rank. Quakers honor the testimony of equality and made a point to address all in the same way. Now, though, the use of *thee* in the common parlance has given way to *you*, yet the Society of Friends maintains the old style."

I heard a clop-clop-clop on the pavement behind us and turned to see Bertie Winslow ride up on her horse. She was postmistress of our town of Amesbury, and as unconventional a spirit as I'd ever met.

"Whoa up, Grover," she called, pulling on the reins. She carried a basket on her lap.

Only Bertie would name a horse "Grover." I always smiled to hear her refer to a large animal by the name of our country's president. It was delightfully subversive. And only Bertie had the nerve to ride astride instead of sidesaddle. She slid a leg over Grover's back and hopped off the animal. As she tied him to the tree, the hem of her skirt fell down over her bloomers. The bloomers, made from a cloth that matched the skirt, always showed when she rode. Bertie didn't care what people thought.

"I bring sustenance," she announced, and plopped down on the cloth with us. "How is my favorite Quaker midwife? And the bearer of the new human?"

"I am well," I said. "But Helen is ailing a bit, I'm afraid."

Bertie frowned. "Come and eat, then. My picnics can cure anything." She set to drawing paper-wrapped packets and two bottles out of the basket. "See here? Cold meat pies, dilly beans, berry tarts, even a bottle of ale." She glanced at me. "And lemonade for our teetotaler Rose."

Helen hoisted herself up onto her elbows and then to sitting, her knees to one side. "My stomach is unsettled, as well."

"Did thee eat this morning?" I asked.

"Oh, yes." Helen smiled. "Rupert always fixes my breakfast. But I'll take a little ale to settle myself."

Bertie poured a metal cup of ale for Helen and for herself, and handed me a portion of tangy lemonade. "I saw your husband in the post office this morning," she said to Helen, raising her perfectly arched eyebrows as she unpinned her hat and threw it on the cloth.

When Helen reached for her cup, her loose sleeve fell back, revealing a dark patch on her forearm. She pulled her sleeve down and her smile turned nervous. "Rupert told me he had a parcel to send. I don't know what it was."

Bertie pressed her lips together and didn't comment. I bit into a meat pie, thinking that patch on Helen's arm looked a lot like a bruise.

"Mmm, perfect crust, delicious filling," I said once I swallowed. "Thank thee, Bertie."

We ate and chatted for most of an hour, although Helen nibbled more than ate. A family picnicked a little ways down and we watched as the children splashed in the water. A song sparrow entertained us from a nearby bush while a breeze brought a semblance of water-scented coolness off the lake, which was really just the Powow River backed up behind the Salisbury Mills dam.

Bertie rose with a sigh. "Back to work for me. My employees always come up with some trouble for me to solve when I'm away for too long."

After I tidied the food and repacked Bertie's basket, I handed it up to her on Grover and waved farewell.

"And we have your antenatal appointment, Helen." I tied my bonnet back on, then gave Helen a hand up to standing. We strolled the few blocks to my office in the front parlor of the house I shared with my brother-in-law and his five children. I still suffered a pang of longing every time I approached the house, despite my pride in seeing the shingle announcing Rose Carroll, Midwife hanging out front. The pain of missing my late sister had not lessened in the two years since her death.

I made Helen comfortable on my examination chaise, then brought each of us a glass of water. We went through the arrangements for when her time came.

"Who will thee have to help thee at home?"

"My mother will come for as long as I need her. My family is in Newbury, so it's not far."

"Excellent. Next time I'll come and see thee at home to make sure all will be ready, in case the child decides to come early." After I took her pulse, I said, "I'll need to palpate the baby today, Helen. Is thee ready?"

She nodded. She lifted her skirts, holding them up under her armpits, and pulled her drawers down below her belly. Her ribs on one side bore a yellowing bruise. I touched it gently.

"What happened here?"

She didn't meet my eyes as she said, "I was clumsy. I ran into the corner of the bureau."

"Is that what happened to thy arm, as well?" I pulled her sleeve back.

This time she looked straight at me. "Yes." Her voice was defiant but she blinked away a tear.

I busied myself with measuring the length from her pubic bone to the top of the womb. With the Pinard horn pressed against her belly, I tracked the baby's heartbeat. Manipulating gently with my hands, I felt the baby's head and bottom to assess its size. I checked Helen's ankles. While not overly swollen, they showed a yellow cast to the skin.

"Thee can restore thy coverings now," I said, turning to my desk to jot down my findings. I faced her again. "Thee can feel safe with me, Helen. Is thy husband beating thee?" If he was, there was nothing I could do except hope to keep her and her baby safe. Our local police took the position that what happened in a marriage was the business of the man and his wife, not the authorities.

She gazed at me with dark eyes. "Sometimes he gets carried away. But he loves me. He tells me so. And he watches out for me, truly. I told you he makes me breakfast every day."

I sighed inwardly. How many times had I heard that? Once it was from a client who ended up dead at the hands of the man who she declared loved her.

"Has he always made the morning meal?"

"No, just for the last month." Helen squeezed her eyes shut and grimaced.

As she did, I noticed that her face also bore a faint yellowish tint. "Thee is having another headache."

She nodded. "I think I'd better go see your doctor, after all. What was his name?"

"Good. His name is David Dodge. Let us go across the river." I checked the mantel clock that had been my grandmother's, which read two-thirty. "David holds office hours at the new Anna Jaques Hospital in Newburyport all afternoon. I'll have thee home in time to make supper. Put thy hat on and come along." I was glad I was free to accompany her. She was my only antenatal appointment for the afternoon. The children were spending the summer on my parents' farm in Lawrence, and my brother-in-law had told me he was dining with friends that evening.

I bustled us both out of the house and we went looking for a conveyance for hire on High Street.

"I'll need a small lock of your hair," David told Helen when he was finished examining her. It had taken us twenty minutes to find a hack, we'd had to wait a bit to see David, and he had taken care with his examination, so it was now getting on for five o'clock.

"Why?" Helen asked, taken aback.

"Just to aid in assessing your health," David said, slipping me a look behind Helen's back. He handed her a small pair of scissors.

Helen shrugged, but handed the scissors to me. I clipped off a small bit from near her neckline and handed the deep brown lock to David, along with the scissors.

"Thank you for coming in," he said. "I'll have an answer for you within a day's time. And Rose, thanks for bringing her. I'll summon my carriage and driver to take you both back to Amesbury."

"That's very kind of thee," I said.

"I'll need to use the outhouse before we leave." Helen blushed a little.

"Oh, we have the new chain-pull toilets," David said with a note of pride in his voice. "The lavatory is just down the hall to the right. It's labeled Ladies." He pointed the way.

After the door closed behind Helen, I gave him a quizzical glance.

"My teacher in medical school would call it gastric fever." He gazed at me. "I suspect poison."

"Poison?" I whispered, moving to his side.

"Arsenic. I'll tell you for certain after I've analyzed the hair." His brows knitted, he went on, "Don't tell her. Yet."

After David's driver dropped Helen at her home, I had him leave me at Bertie's house. She would be closing up at the post office about now and I wanted to talk this business through with her. We'd been friends for several years. She was ten years older than I, but although she was nearing forty, her energy for both fun and justice never flagged. We were neither of us married and she felt like a kindred spirit. Some in town muttered about her being in a so-called Boston Marriage with her friend Sophie, with whom she shared the cheerful cottage I now stood in front of. I knew she had strong feelings for Sophie, who traveled so much for her work that Bertie and I had time for our friendship. That was their business, not mine.

I wandered through the riot of color that was her front garden, a tangle of flowers and greenery in a controlled chaos of all hues and shapes. I found a watering can and gave a drink to several pots of wilting pansies.

Sure enough, up Bertie clattered on Grover not five minutes later. She jumped down. "What, blessed with another Rosetta visit so soon? Come with me while I put this man in his quarters."

I followed her back to the shed that doubled as stable. I lounged on a bench under an enormous elm tree to watch as she wiped Grover down and gave him fresh water along with his portion of oats. Her small back garden was shady, welcoming, and smelled deliciously of the sweet peas trained up the shed wall. When she was done, Bertie sank onto the bench next to me.

"I fear for Helen's life," I said. I told her of the bruises, and of David's guess as to the cause of her symptoms. "She acknowledged her husband gets a little carried away, as she put it, but says he loves her. But if he is adding a small dose of arsenic to her breakfast each day, he's killing her. Likely her child, as well. What kind of monster would do that?"

"A bigot and a philanderer, that's who," Bertie exclaimed. "Rupert Stillwell is rotten through and through. He mailed a package this morning, all right. The box was from Adelia's Fine Clothing and it was addressed to a Miss Chartreuse LeVesque."

I whistled. "I'd guess she's not his little sister."

"I'd agree. Yet you should see the looks he gives me. I hear him sniggering to his friends about Sophie and me. You know I don't care what people say, but for a miserable rat like him to think he's better than we are, that gets my goat."

"*Rat.*" I stared at her. "Rat poison contains arsenic. What shall we do to make him stop?"

Bertie sighed. "What we *should* do is tell Amesbury's finest. This is a job for the police, not for us."

"Thee knows they don't care if men beat their wives. And they'd have to prove he is giving Helen poison."

"Unlikely to happen." She shook her head. "I think it's going to be up to you and me, Miss Carroll."

I was called to a birth the next morning. It was blessedly uncomplicated, being the third baby born to a well-nourished mother who lived in a house with clean running water. As I arrived home, the afternoon post brought a note from David. His tests confirmed his hypothesis. I freshened up and headed for the post office. It was time to put the plan Bertie and I had hatched into motion.

Detective Kevin Donovan knocked at my door the next morning at nine o'clock exactly. I greeted him and invited him into the parlor.

"Miss Carroll, I understand that Helen Stillwell was under your care." The robust police officer stood with his hat in his hands.

"She still is, Kevin." I cocked my head. "Won't thee sit down?"

He cringed a little at my use of his first name. We'd had prior contact, however, and he knew that Friends did not believe in using titles for anyone, not even for the authorities.

"No, I'll stay on my feet, thank you."

"I examined her only two days ago," I went on. "Her baby is due in approximately two months."

"Was she despondent? Anxious, perhaps?"

"A bit, but at that stage most first-time mothers are. The act of giving birth is dangerous for mothers and babies alike. She was having some other health problems, though. Headaches, dizzy spells, some stomach distress."

He waved that off. "You don't think she would harm herself?"

"Why does thee ask?" I folded my hands in my lap.

"She left her husband a note. Said she couldn't stand it any more, and was going for a swim in the lake. Forever, as she put it."

I gasped and put a hand to my mouth. "Does thee mean she drowned herself?"

"I'm afraid so. She is nowhere to be found, and we located her hat and handkerchief near the bluff overlooking the lake. There is the note, too."

"I heard the emergency bell tolling last evening." I shook my head in sorrow.

"Yes, Rupert Stillwell came to us just after dark with the note. He's distraught, as you can imagine."

"If only I had detected the signs." I shook my head. "Will thee be dragging the lake?"

"Likely not. It looks to be a pretty clear case. And bodies usually surface in a few days, unless they are weighted down," Kevin said. "Such a pity, a young thing like that, and their baby dead, too."

"Is there a possibility that the note is a forgery? Perhaps someone, even her husband, wanted Helen dead."

"What an imagination you have, Rose Carroll," he scoffed. "You think a pregnant woman was murdered? In Amesbury?"

I shrugged. "One wishes it not to be so, but people are murdered. Thee knows that better than I."

"This is no murder." He placed his hat on his head. "I'll be going now."

"I shall stop by and see if I can be of assistance to Rupert," I called as Kevin made his way down the front steps.

An hour later I knocked on Rupert's door. The apartment occupied the upper floor of a house down by Clark's Pond. He flung it open with a hopeful look on his face, which fell immediately upon seeing me.

"Rupert," I said, taking his hand in both of mine. "I am so sorry to hear about poor Helen's disappearance. What a sorrow for thee."

He stared. "You're the midwife," he finally said. His hair was neatly combed back and he wore a clean collar, but his tie was askew and his shirt misbuttoned.

I nodded. "I am Rose Carroll. May I come in?"

"Of course." He hesitated for a moment, then stood back and let me pass.

The door opened onto a kitchen in great disarray. The sink overflowed with dirty dishes. On the table the open newspaper vied with a plate of dried eggs, a tipped-over salt shaker, and a cup holding coffee mixed with flecks of curdled cream. Crumbs filled the cracks in the wide pine floor. No wonder he gave pause to letting me enter.

"I was just about to go out," he said. "Those police say they ain't going to drag Lake Gardner for my Helen. They have to!" He wrung his hands.

"May I offer to help thee? I can at least clean up the kitchen here, while thee is out."

"Oh, would you, Miss Carroll? Helen wasn't the best of housekeepers, and I'm hopeless, myself." Rupert jammed his hat on his head. "How can I hold a funeral without her body?" He walked through the still open doorway and clattered down the stairs.

I shut the door and got to work.

By the time the noon whistle pierced the air, Rupert had a spotless kitchen and I was walking into C.L. & J.W. Allen's Hardware on Market Square. JW himself greeted me.

"Friend Carroll, what can we do for you today?" He beamed

from behind the counter.

I drew the slip of paper I'd found in Helen's apartment out of my bag. "My client Helen Stillwell bought this rat poison from thee in May. I was thinking of getting some of the same brand, in case rats come around our place."

He peered at the receipt through his reading glasses. "Oh, no," he said, looking at me over the top of the spectacles. "That was Rupert himself who purchased the arsenic. Said his wife told him they had quite the infestation."

"I see. Arsenic is very toxic, isn't it?"

"Yes, indeed. You'll want to be very careful with it."

I pursed my lips. "I think I'll wait, then, since we're not having a rodent problem at present. Wouldn't want the children getting into a poison."

He nodded gravely.

"I thank thee," I said, retrieving the receipt, and walked back into the busy square. Carriages and drays vied with the people of the town walking up Friend Street, down Main Street, coming in from Elm, heading out on Market, running for the train on Water. I made my way carefully up Main to the police station.

Inside, I asked for the detective and perched on a waiting bench, my toe tapping the marble floor. Kevin emerged into the lobby and stood with legs splayed, arms crossed. He didn't look happy.

"Miss Carroll, what is it now?"

I stood. "Kevin, I request a moment of thy time. I have evidence to show that not only was Rupert Stillwell beating his wife, he was also slowly killing her with poison. Thee must arrest him."

His eyes bugged open. "But his wife is dead by her own hand. And her mother showed up here wailing and nearly rending her garments."

"I don't believe that Helen killed herself. Must I show thee what I have here in the lobby for all to see?" In fact, a gentleman looking down on his luck watched us with great interest from the facing bench.

Grumbling, the detective led the way into his office. Unbidden, I sat in the only chair not burdened with books or papers. Kevin leaned against his desk. I drew several items out of my bag and began.

"First, at my last examination of Helen Stillwell on Monday, I noticed bruises on her arm and her ribs. She admitted that her husband beats her."

Kevin rolled his eyes. "Haven't we been through the legal status on this? My hands are tied."

"Second, she was complaining of physical symptoms not related to pregnancy. Doctor David Dodge of Newburyport gave her a thorough examination, also on Monday. He sampled her hair. The results were positive for arsenic poisoning in the last month." I waved the note from David as he opened his mouth. "It's here in writing. Third, she told me her husband has been making her breakfast every day for a month."

"Isn't that nice of him?"

I'd never heard Kevin so sarcastic. "Fourth, J.W. Allen himself examined this receipt and said that Rupert bought this rat poison—arsenic—in May." I laid the receipt on the desk. "Fifth, Rupert was seen mailing a package from a ladies' fine clothing store to a woman not his wife. And finally, thee will find in this packet the remains of cooked eggs and other breakfast foods from the Stillwell kitchen. I fully expect that they contain a portion of arsenic. Thee must find Rupert Stillwell and arrest him. I am convinced he wanted to get rid of his pregnant wife so he could marry his mistress."

He gave a grudging nod. "You seem to have a case. But what about the matter of the missing Helen? If he was poisoning her, why should she kill herself?" He rubbed his forehead. "Her body has not come to the surface of the lake. Should be appearing soon, maybe tomorrow."

"Rupert could have drowned her, and weighted her down. Or perhaps she didn't drown at all. She could have just wanted to get away, especially since he was hitting her. Maybe she went to a friend."

"It's true, without a body, we have no proof of her death. Either way, I will have the food tested, and Mr. Allen's story confirmed. I guess I should thank you for doing my work for me." He smiled. "Now get on with you and leave me to it."

The last post the next afternoon brought the news I awaited. I walked through Bertie's front gate at close to six o'clock just as she rode up. I waited while she tied the horse to an iron ring in the hitching post. As we entered the kitchen, Helen glanced up from the bread she was kneading. Flour dusted the apron she wore loosely tied around her girth and a white smudge decorated her forehead.

"Any news?" she asked with a hopeful look.

I glanced at Bertie. "Yes," I said, smiling. "Rupert has been arrested for poisoning. The detective found the arsenic in the remains of thy breakfast and in the salt shaker. Thee is safe now, Helen, both from the poison and from his abuse."

"And his philandering, don't forget. I'm so grateful to you both," Helen said with a sigh. "And I already feel much better, going a couple of days without it."

"Good. Ale to celebrate?" Bertie asked as she flopped down in a chair.

"Thank you, but I should probably be getting home," Helen said. "My mother must be worried sick."

"What will thee tell the townsfolk?" I removed my bonnet and wiped perspiration from my brow. The heat had not relented.

"That I needed to get away for a bit. That I was pretending in that note." She rolled the lump of dough under the heels of her hands and then slapped the top of it. "I am grateful to you both for rescuing me when you did. Even though I framed him, of course."

Bertie and I exchanged a glance. "What do you mean, framed him?" Bertie asked.

"I arranged for the arsenic to go in my own breakfast. Told Rupert it was a special pregnancy salt he had to shake onto my eggs. Didn't touch the shaker, myself, once I'd filled it and wiped it clean. I couldn't think of any other way to get clear of him, with his mistresses and his beating me. Don't worry, I'd read up on the dose. I was never going to kill myself." She removed the apron, dusted off her hands, and grabbed her hat from the tree. "Thank you again. I'll see you around town."

The door closed behind her. Bertie and I stared at each other in horror. Helen poisoning herself was one thing. Putting a near-term baby at risk was quite another.

"I'm heading directly to the police station," I said, anger making my voice shake. "And thee?"

"I'll take you on Grover." Bertie's eyes flashed as she strode out the door. "Nobody dupes Bertie Winslow."

The Management of Secrets

Author Note: Here we find Rose Carroll ten years after *A Changing Light,* the last book in the Quaker Midwife Mysteries series. She has retired from crime solving but not from midwifery, but Kevin Donovan persuades her to take on one more case.

Keeping a secret can be destructive, at times criminal. Midwife Rose Dodge knew it sometimes was an act of kindness.

Despite this being the first month in a new year in a new century, Rose mused that 1900 didn't seem much different from 1899, at least not here in the northeast corner of Massachusetts. The electric trolley still ran. The government still functioned. The newspapers and the milk were still delivered. And women still needed assistance with their pregnancies and births.

A knocking sounded on her office door, the entrance separate from the family's. It was likely a distraught husband fetching her for his wife's labor. She smiled after she pulled it open to see Police Chief Kevin Donovan, instead. She'd worked closely with him a decade earlier, helping to solve a number of tricky murder cases.

"Kevin, do come in. What a delight to see thee." She stepped back. "That is, unless something is amiss with a member of my family." Her smile slid away, and she brought her hand to her mouth.

"Oh, no, Miss Rose, I've no reports of harm to your beloveds." He moved into her office, holding his hat in his hands. "Would you listen to me, now? I can't help calling you Miss

Rose, despite you being a married lady and mother to four babies."

"I don't care a bit. It's rather fun to think of the days when I was a 'Miss.' Sit down and tell me the news."

"Look. I know you gave up detecting when your first wee girl was born, and rightly so. But I'm faced with a case that's got my head in a bother, and it seems to cross paths with your own life in more than one way."

"I hope one of my expectant ladies hasn't been murdered nor is suspected of committing homicide."

"Well, no." He rubbed his round head, his carrot-colored hair now shot through with the silver of a man nearing fifty years. "But there might be a lady with child involved. And one of your Quaker gents, too."

"Goodness. What crime is thee investigating?"

"Seems a good deal of counterfeit bills are circulating in Amesbury of late. This fellow, Thomas Franklin, appears to be connected with the offense."

"He's a fellow member of the Religious Society of Friends, it's true." Rose pictured Tom, a handsome accountant not much older than her thirty-seven years. He was married to a pinched-looking woman named Ida, but they had no children. "How is he connected?"

"Edwin Sawyer, the grocer, thinks it was Franklin who used one of the tens for his purchase. Him or his wife."

"Interesting. And who is the pregnant woman?"

"Name's Mrs. Penelope McPherson."

"She's a client of mine, in fact. A recent widow, if memory serves, about halfway through her term."

"Yes, her husband was killed in an accident. He owned the printing company over on Market Street," Kevin said.

"And she owns it now." Rose's thoughts swirled.

"Yes. Why's it so quiet around here, by the way?"

"What?" Rose blinked. "Oh, our nanny, Marie-Fleur, took Davey and Herbie off to play with their cousins. Hattie and Clara are in school. And Dr. Dodge is either in his office downtown or seeing patients at the Methodist Hospital."

"Four-year-old twin boys have to be a handful, Miss Rose."

"They are. Thank goodness for Marie-Fleur. She has the patience of one of thy saints. It's never quiet here for long, though, and I expected thy knock to be news of a woman in labor." Rose tapped her desk. "Tell me, where else has this counterfeit money been appearing, and what marks it as fake?"

"It shows up here and there in town, including at the post office. Your Miss Winslow first brought it to our attention."

"Bertie's always had a sharp eye." Rose smiled again. Her irreverent friend had been postmistress for many years. "I'll stop by and see her."

Kevin pulled out a ten-dollar greenback. "As for how you can tell, see here?" He pointed to a spot on the front. "This bill is good. But on the fakes, they didn't get this part of the bison quite right."

Rose nodded. "Is it all denominations?"

"No, just the tens. We've quietly alerted Amesbury merchants to check for the forgeries and asked them to put aside any counterfeits they come across. Somebody's keeping a big secret, and it's not good for anyone." He cleared his throat and stood. "I'd appreciate whatever nosing around you can do, Miss Rose, as long as you stay safe doing it. We can't be having our money system tampered with."

"I'll do what I can. Give my love to the family." She clicked the door shut behind him and leaned against it. She couldn't deny the frisson of excitement at being involved in a case again. She had a rich, full life, with her family and her work. But investigating crimes? She knew she had a gift for it. As long as it didn't interfere with her obligations, she didn't see any reason not to help Kevin in his pursuit. It wasn't as if she'd be in danger from a murderer.

***

"If it isn't the Quaker midwife, herself," Bertie exclaimed half an hour later from behind the counter of the post office. Bertie's curly blond hair was now mixed with white, but her cheery face remained nearly unlined, and her petite figure was as trim as ever in a crisp shirtwaist and dark skirt.

"Good morning, my friend." Rose glanced around. Only two people waited in line to mail parcels. "Might I have a word with thee in private?"

"Eva, I'll be in my office," Bertie said to her assistant.

"Yes, Miss Winslow."

"What's on your mind, Rosetta?" Bertie asked a moment later, using the nickname she'd invented.

"Kevin has asked me to assist in the matter of the counterfeit money."

"From the sparkle in your eye, I'd say you're delighted to be back in business, so to speak."

"Thee knows me too well. I'm experiencing a bit of a thrill, yes." Rose gave a nod. "He said thee was the first to bring the forgery to the attention of the police. What made you notice a fake bill?"

"Well, I was counting the day's money on Monday, and something was off about the feel of that ten. Look." Bertie extracted an envelope from her desk drawer and pulled out a ten-dollar bill. "The paper's not quite right. I took a magnifying glass to it and spied the tail of the mighty bison was not the same as on a real tenner. There are other miniscule bits that are wrong." She pointed here and there.

"Today is Sixth Day, so only five days have elapsed. Does thee have any idea who paid with this bill?"

"No, more's the pity, and neither does Eva. We get pretty

busy here."

"I won't take any more of thy time. I'm off to visit a lady who owns a printing press, and then to hunt down a fellow Quaker."

"You think Mrs. McPherson might be the culprit?" Bertie arched an eyebrow.

"I pray not. She's carrying her late husband's child. But sometimes the simplest solutions are the correct ones." Rose touched her friend's shoulder. "Thee and Sophie should come to dinner tomorrow. My Davey is mad about the mail. He's forever scribbling on papers, folding them into packets, and pretending to send them. He's crushed if he misses the postman. And Clara, at seven, has already declared she plans to become a lady lawyer like Auntie Sophie."

"I'll ask her. Good luck in your hunt."

***

Rose pulled open the door to McPherson Printing on Market Street twenty minutes later. The office was warm and busy with a young man leaning over a drawing board and a sturdy matron tying a brown-paper-wrapped parcel with string. Penelope sat behind a desk writing in a ledger. From the back came the rhythmic clatter of a press, but the noise was muffled by a closed door.

Penelope glanced up. "Why, hello, Mrs. Dodge. What can I do for you?" Her hand strayed to the bulge of her five-month pregnant belly, as if having a midwife walk in had brought her growing baby to mind. Her dark good looks were enhanced by the heightened color of her condition.

"Good morning, Penelope." Rose had thought up an excuse as she'd walked. "I'd like to have cards printed for my sons."

"A child's calling card?"

"Yes. The twins are only four, but their sisters have cards, and my little Herbie is a serious sort who would quite like something so formal."

"Please sit down. You'll want something small and simple, I

assume?"

"Certainly." Rose sat.

Penelope slid a piece of paper and a pencil across to her. "Write their names clearly."

Rose carefully printed David Allan Dodge and Herbert Wesley Dodge and slid the paper back to Penelope. "Those names make them sound like grown men." She smiled.

"As they will be before long." Penelope checked a big calendar on the wall next to her, its squares filled with what looked to be job descriptions. "The order will be ready in a week's time. We have a number of pieces ahead of yours on the schedule."

"Thee seems to be doing a good business here. Was it terribly difficult learning to run it?" Rose had had only one antenatal visit with Penelope, and they hadn't talked about her work. Her client was only twenty-three. Rose was impressed by her competence.

"I'd worked alongside my husband, so it wasn't hard to take charge of the operation."

Rose leaned forward. "Did thee hear there is counterfeit money circulating in Amesbury? I find the news shocking."

Penelope blinked at the change of topic. "It is. Counterfeiting is a federal offense."

"The government certainly caught Emmanuel Ninger for the crime not that long ago. What would be involved in printing false bills?" Rose didn't have to feign ignorance. Creating fake currency was completely outside her experience. "Don't they take a special type of paper?"

"I believe they do. Beyond that, I wouldn't have the slightest notion how to even begin." She didn't meet Rose's gaze.

Rose expected Penelope might have much more than a slight notion about how to print counterfeit money. The door to the back opened, and the noise level rose considerably. A dark-haired man in a long black apron pushed through and let the door swing shut behind him. Rose's eyes widened. What was Tom Franklin doing working as a printer?

"Penny, do—" he began but halted when he spied Rose. "Mrs. McPherson, I've got a bit of a problem back there."

Penelope flushed as she turned to look at him. The matron lifted her head from her work and gazed from her pretty employer to the handsome printer.

"Hello, Tom." Rose stood. "I didn't know thee worked here."

"Good morning, Rose," he said, his dark brows coming together over striking green eyes. "Yes, I do."

The noon whistle went off outside, signaling a lunch break for the many mill and factory workers downtown.

"I'll be getting along," Rose said. "I thank thee, Penelope, and I'll see thee next week. Good day, Tom." Outside, she glanced back through the window as Penelope disappeared into the back room with Tom.

***

Holding Hattie's mittened hand, Rose trudged along Whittier Street through freshly fallen snow the two blocks to the Friends Meetinghouse on First Day morning. She'd been called to a birth last evening just as a delightful dinner with Bertie, Sophie, and the family had been winding down.

It was the third child for the birthing woman, with a speedy and easy labor and the appearance of a healthy baby girl. This morning Rose had had time for bite to eat at home, a wash, and a two-hour nap before it was time to leave for worship. David, who usually attended the Unitarian service in Newburyport, opted not to go today. He offered to keep the children with him, but Hattie had insisted on accompanying her mother.

"I like being quiet, Mama," she'd said.

Rose didn't blame her, being eldest of four. It was rarely quiet in their busy home. Rose would have stayed home, herself, except she was now Clerk of the Women's Business Meeting, and today was the day they gathered.

At least the storm had passed quickly. Now sunlight danced off crystals of snow, and the air was crisp and clean.

"Mama, does thee think I should become a doctor or a midwife when I'm older?" Hattie asked.

"Thee will find the path that suits thee. Thee would excel at either occupation."

"I think we need more lady doctors."

"We do, at that."

Inside the simple white Meetinghouse, Rose slid into a pew on the left side.

"I'm going to go sit with Rosie," Hattie whispered.

Rose smiled and nodded, watching as Hattie nearly skipped to the other side to squeeze in with her cousin, only eight months younger, whom Rose's niece had named for her. Rose shut her eyes.

But, in the stillness, her mind raced back to the case of the counterfeit money, which she had put aside in favor of family yesterday. Were Tom and Penelope secretly working together to illegally print greenbacks? Were they, instead, having an illicit dalliance? Maybe it was both. How could she find out?

She eased her eyes open. Tom and Ida sat across the room under one of the eight-foot-tall windows. Ida, hands folded in her lap and eyes closed, had raised her face to the sun streaming in the opposite window. The light softened her usually tight expression. Tom's eyes flew open as if he'd felt Rose's gaze, and he narrowed them at her. She gave him a little smile before returning to what she'd come here for, an hour of silent prayer and expectant waiting on God.

***

After the rise of Meeting, Hattie ran up and asked if she could go home with Rosie.

"We're going to go sledding." Hattie's eyes sparkled. "Auntie

Faith said she'll bring me home in time for supper."

"Go and have fun." Rose kissed her daughter's head and sent her along, then headed over to the right side of the building as a ponderous creaking began. Friends raised the partition between the two halves of the meetinghouse to let the women conduct their business independently from the men.

Ida helped Rose move a table into place in front of the facing bench. Rose laid her papers and pen on the table and sat, folding her hands and closing her eyes. She sensed Ida sitting down next to her. The gradual stilling of the room was something to be savored. Women hurried in and took their places on the pews. Footsteps ceased. Breathing slowed. The men did the same on the other side.

After a few minutes of silent prayer, Rose opened her eyes. "We gather on this seventh day of First Month in worship with attention to the women's business of Amesbury Monthly Meeting of Friends. Will our Recording Clerk please relay the minutes from Twelfth Month?"

Ida read the minutes in her thin voice. And the meeting went along, with the women discussing a wedding, hospitality, and a memorial Meeting to honor a Friend who'd died of tuberculosis. At the same time, the low rumble of male timbres drifted through the divider as they conducted their own business.

Ida's bony fingers scribed the minutes. She had dirt under her fingernails, which seemed odd, but perhaps she nurtured plants through the winter on sunny windowsills or in a greenhouse.

In the back of her mind, Rose mused on how much younger and prettier Penelope was than this angular woman who rarely smiled. She remembered how Penelope had flushed at seeing Tom come out from the printing room, and how he'd called her Penny. If he, rather than her late husband, was the father of Penelope's baby, keeping the paternity secret from Ida might grow more difficult in time.

Rose gathered her papers after the meeting was over and turned to Ida. "I saw Tom working at McPherson Printing recently. How long has he been in their employ?"

"He's worked there since Arthur McPherson's soul was released to God in Ninth Month. *She* needed someone." Ida's mouth twisted at the word "she."

"Tom was an accountant at the Merrimack Hat Factory, wasn't he? That's quite a change in profession."

"He was, but they let him go." She shrugged. "Both our fathers were printers. That's how we met. Tom knows the business."

The silence on the other side of the partition ceased, with boot heels thudding and male voices growing louder.

"The men are finished," Ida said. "I need to get along, Rose. Tom doesn't like his dinner to be late."

Rose nodded, watching her go. She thought she might want to spend some time in the public library tomorrow. How exactly had McPherson died? And why had Tom been fired from the factory?

***

Stretching out a crick in her neck the next morning, Rose gazed around the cramped little library. John Greenleaf Whittier had been a founding member and had donated many of the original books. But with the growth in the town's industry, so had the population grown. Ground was being broken later this year for a much-needed new building. For now, she had to settle for the small table she'd covered with the newspapers from last fall.

She couldn't find a word about Tom's being let go, which didn't surprise her, but the firing itself did. The hat factory employed several hundred men and women and was a thriving business. He must have been negligent in some way to have lost his job.

About Arthur McPherson's death, Rose gleaned a bit more. He was forty-five, considerably older than Penelope. He'd died at the beginning of Ninth Month. His horse was spooked and took the open buggy McPherson was driving down Whittier Hill at such a rate that the conveyance overturned near an outcropping of rock. The driver, alone in the buggy, was dead by the time the ambulance wagon arrived. Details about what had startled the horse and what McPherson was doing atop Whittier Hill were not included.

Rose folded the papers and returned them to their shelf. It was time for a visit to the police station.

***

"Kevin," she began once she was seated across from the chief in his office. "What does thee know about the circumstances surrounding Arthur McPherson's death?"

"Why, it was a runaway horse."

"But what spooked the steed?" The Grand Hotel sat atop Whittier Hill, which meant all kinds of people came and went in the course of a day. "Did thee investigate who was about at the top of the hill?"

"Not that I know of." Kevin peered at her. "Are you thinking the accident was caused purposeful, like?"

"I don't know."

"I can't believe one of your peaceable Quakers would commit a violent act, Miss Rose."

"Sadly, criminals have been known to exist even among Friends. We are all human, after all. What I do know is that Tom Franklin was fired from his job as an accountant with the Merrimack Hat Factory. His wife, Ida, told me it happened about the time of Arthur McPherson's demise."

"You don't say."

"I do. Tom's now working as a printer for Penelope McPherson. In addition, when I stopped in there on Sixth Day, owner and employee seemed overly affectionate."

Kevin whistled. "And the two might have conspired to get Mr. McPherson out of the way. But Franklin's a married man?"

She looked at him over her spectacles. "When has that prevented many a male from dallying with women younger and prettier than their wives?"

"True enough."

Should she raise the possibility of who had fathered Penelope's baby? Not now. The only way to know for sure was to ask the mother-to-be.

"Also," she continued, "Tom is an experienced printer. I should think between the two of them, he and Penelope might be thy counterfeiters."

"I need proof, though."

"Indeed. Does thee have men watching the press at night?"

"Not yet, but I'll put someone on it, and have patrolmen canvass the neighborhood, as well," Kevin said. "We're shorthanded, or I would have thought of it myself. At least McPherson's is the only printer in town."

"The business appears to be doing well, but perhaps it's not. Creating her own funds might have seemed like a solution to Penelope."

"Or to Tom Franklin, after he was fired. He could be doing it secretly, without Mrs. McPherson's knowledge, in order to support himself and his wife."

Rose glanced at the clock. "I need to be getting home. Thee will see what thee can learn about the horse and buggy accident. I'll have a chat with Penelope."

"With your help, we'll get these criminals shut down. Thank you for agreeing to investigate."

***

"I'm glad thee came in," Rose said to Penelope at one o'clock that afternoon as the pregnant woman reclined on the examination chaise in Rose's office. "Thee was overdue for a second visit."

"Thank you for your note. I didn't realize I needed to see you again before my labor begins."

Rose had clearly outlined the schedule of care at Penelope's first visit, but she didn't scold her for the lapse. And if Rose was able to learn something about Penelope and Tom, so much the better.

"Thee can pull down thy skirts," Rose said when she was finished measuring and palpating Penelope's belly. She checked her file. "At thy first visit, thee said thy last monthly began on the second of August. Is thee sure?" Rose used conventional day of the week and month names with her clients even though Quakers avoided them so they didn't invoke the memory of gods and emperors.

"I'm pretty sure." Penelope fidgeted with the cuff of her sleeve, not meeting Rose's gaze. "Does it matter?"

"It's rather important to gauge when thee will deliver. The baby seems small for being this far along. Is thee eating enough nourishing foods?"

"Why, yes, I have a hearty appetite."

"If the date is correct, the fetus might be failing to thrive."

Penelope kneaded her hands in her lap, frowning at them. She let out a long breath and raised her face.

"Oh, Mrs. Dodge. I'm in a terrible pickle. You are a wise midwife and correct about my condition. Since Arthur died, I have become intimate with Tom Franklin."

"And the baby is his."

"Yes," she said, her dark eyes brimming. "I know how wrong it is. But I was desperately unhappy with Arthur. He was so old, and he was neither kind nor sweet with me. All he wanted was someone to work for free and to give him an heir." She cradled her belly.

"I do not judge, Penelope. But please be truthful. I suspect thee was intimate with Tom before Arthur's accident."

"Not intimate, but we wanted to be," Penelope whispered. "Please don't tell a soul."

Rose couldn't promise to keep her secret. "Are thee and Tom printing counterfeit bills?"

Penelope gaped. "What? Of course not. Why would I do something like that?"

"Perhaps he is, without thy knowledge." Rose raised her eyebrows. "In secret."

"No." Penelope gave her head a firm shake. "He never would."

Maybe. Or maybe not.

***

At four o'clock, Rose knocked on the door of Tom and Ida's cottage. She'd enlisted Bertie to drive her down there and wait in her carriage. Rose hadn't let Ida know she was coming.

"Rose?" Ida, frowning, gave a furtive glance over her own shoulder. "What brings thee here?"

"I'd like to talk with thee about a matter that has arisen." Rose patted the satchel she'd brought and held her breath, hoping Ida would assume the visit was about Quaker women's affairs.

"Yes?" Ida didn't budge from the threshold.

"May I come in? It's chilly out here."

Ida swallowed. "Very well. Let's go straight back to the kitchen, and I'll fix tea."

Rose followed her, leaving the door ajar an inch. She slipped off one glove and slid her hand into her cloak pocket as she paused at the door to a study. On a drop-front desk next to a window bare of curtains lay pens, paper, a sheet of metal, a magnifying glass on a stand, and various sharp-looking tools. A gas lamp with a clear shade was turned up high.

"Is thee creating art?" Rose strove to keep her voice casual. She stepped into the room.

Ida whirled. "What are you doing in there?" With two long strides she was at Rose's side.

"Ida, I believe thee is part of Tom's counterfeiting scheme. I'm sure the police will be lenient if thee tells them what he's up to."

"That philandering coward?" Her tone was scornful. "He can barely print, let alone engrave. All he can do is romance that poor girl. I despise the both of them." She grabbed the sharpest of the gravers with one hand and Rose's arm with the other. "No, the operation is mine alone. Pretty soon I'll have enough money to escape this horrid town." She pressed the tool into Rose's neck. "This burin and I won't let you reveal my secret."

Rose took in a deep breath even while feeling the pain of the point piercing her skin, even with her heart thudding like a locomotive. She drew out the big metal police whistle and blew with all her might.

Ida cried out. The burin clattered to the floor. She released Rose and clapped her hands to her ears.

Rose kicked the tool away from Ida's reach. She blew again, and once more, as close to Ida's ear as she could get. Ida turned toward the door. Rose stuck out her foot, catching Ida's ankle.

By the time Bertie hurried in, Rose had tied Ida's hands securely behind her. The counterfeiter struggled and swore like a sailor, but Rose kept her knee in the small of Ida's back.

"Looks like you saved the day, Rosetta." Bertie beamed. "You just happened to have a whistle and sturdy twine in your satchel?"

"A midwife is always prepared, Bertie. Might thee find a length of rope to secure her feet and then go find the nearest policeman?"

***

Kevin himself appeared shortly after Bertie returned with a

young patrolman.

"You've done it again, Miss Rose." He and Rose stepped into the parlor to speak. "I knew you would."

"How did thee get here so quickly?"

"I was already on my way. My man found a neighbor who has trouble sleeping. He spied a thin woman going into the printing shop in the dead of night more than once. From the description, it wasn't Mrs. McPherson."

"No. She is naturally rounded and now even more so."

"What put you onto Mrs. Franklin?" he asked.

"She records the minutes for our Quaker women's business meeting. Yesterday I noticed her dirty fingernails and thought perhaps she was a gardener."

"In January?" Kevin's voice rose.

"Some people nurture plants indoors. But this afternoon I saw Penelope McPherson. She protested mightily that Tom would never counterfeit money, and neither would she. I felt she was telling the truth. As I got to thinking, I remembered Ida had told me her father was a printer, and I wondered if Ida's fingernails were stained with ink, not dirt. I thought I'd pay her a visit to find out."

Kevin furrowed his brow. "More rightly, you should have asked us to make that call."

"I believed she'd let me in more readily than a man in uniform. I happened to take a peek into the study and saw her equipment all laid out. She probably kept it secret by shutting it away in the desk each evening before Tom came home, and she must have used his key late at night to print at Penelope's shop. Let's just say she wasn't happy about my discovery."

"I should say not."

"Anyway, all's well that ends well."

He bobbed his head. "By the way, we found a stable boy up at the hotel who saw an eagle swoop down toward McPherson's buggy. That was what spooked the horse."

"I'm glad it wasn't homicide," Rose said.

He peered at her. "Miss Rose, your neck is bloody. She hurt you!" He pulled out a clean handkerchief and handed it to her. "I never meant for you to endanger your person."

"I thank thee." Rose pressed it to her neck. "It seemed she meant to kill me. But it's just a scratch."

Bertie stepped in. "Did you want me to wait longer, Rose, or will our esteemed Chief of Police be transporting you?"

"I'd be happy to leave now, Bertie, so that I might sup with my brood at home."

As Grover's hoofs clopped up the hill in the gloaming, Rose smiled to herself. She'd solved the case. She'd exposed Ida's criminal secret. And she'd kept herself—and Penelope's secret—safe.

Acknowledgments

I am grateful to every publication that accepted my Quaker Midwife short stories over the years. Level Best Books published the first one, "Breaking the Silence," in 2013 in *Stone Cold: Best New English Crime Stories.* Stories in this collection were published in Bouchercon and Malice Domestic anthologies, in an anthology to benefit the John Greenleaf Whitter Birthplace, in *Kings River Life Magazine*, even in a Texas gardening newsletter. The latest came out in *Deadly Nightshade: Best New England Crime Stories*, from Crime Spell Books in November, 2022. Each editor who wanted my gentle historical crime story helped me release more Rose Carroll tales into the world.

I thank the Al Blanchard Award committee for bestowing an Honorary Mention on "Breaking the Silence" in 2013, and every Malice Domestic attendee who nominated "A Questionable Death" in 2015 and "The Mayor and the Midwife" in 2016 for an Agatha Award for Best Short Story. I didn't bring home an Agatha teapot either of those years, but I applaud winners Art Taylor and Barb Goffman, both masters of the short story. They set a high bar.

Any acknowledgment for stories featuring Rose Carroll must include the late Ramona DeFelice Long. She edited all the Quaker Midwife novels except the last one. Five were nominated for an Agatha Award for Best Historical Novel, and *Charity's Burden* won the prestigious award in 2020. Ramona helped me realize Rose Carroll, Bertie, David, and the other regulars in the series as fuller, deeper characters, which spilled over into the short fiction. She hosted a virtual "sprint club" every morning at seven, which kick-started my writing for the day. She lifted up and encouraged writers everywhere. And she was a friend. I miss you, Ramona, in so many ways.

I am primarily a novelist, but I love writing short fiction. I use it as a break, a palate cleanser, between books. I can explore different voices and different themes, go darker, and have fun with the form. A few years ago, I decided to aim as high as I could. *Alfred Hitchcock Mystery Magazine* and *Ellery Queen Mystery* Magazine have each now published two of my stories, although not any Rose Carroll short fiction.

Thank you so much to Jeffrey Marks and Crippen & Landru for the chance to put these stories together in one volume. I was delighted to add two new shorts: the story about how Rose began sleuthing, as well as the tale of several kinds of labor. I've ended the series of novels but am so pleased to keep my Quaker midwife's presence alive by sharing these accounts of her adventures in both murder and birth.

Always gratitude to the talented Jennifer McKee, who keeps me from having to create my own social media graphics and who helps out with all kinds of authorly project.

To my fellow Amesbury Quakers and the John Greenleaf Whittier Home Association, my Wicked Authors blogmates, the New England and wider Sisters in Crime community, Mystery Writers of America New England, and my close friends and family – thank you all, always, for your support, information, and love.

Edith Maxwell

January 2023

Rose Carroll Sources

"Labor's Peril"—new

"In Pursuit of Justice"—new

"An Ominous Silence." *Snowbound: Best New England Crime Stories 2017* (Level Best Books, 2017).

"The Unfortunate Death of Mrs. Edna Fogg." *Malice Domestic 12: Mystery Most Historical* (Wildside Press, 2017)

"Murder in the Summer Kitchen." *Murder Among Friends: Mysteries Inspired by the Life and Works of John Greenleaf Whittier* (Post Mortem Press, 2017).

"The Mayor and the Midwife." (Agatha Award-nominated) *Blood on the Bayou: Bouchercon Anthology* 2016 (Down and Out Books, 2016).

"Adam and Eva." *Kings River Life Magazine* (2016).

"A Fire in Carriagetown." *Best New England Crime Stories 2014: Stone Cold* (Level Best Books, 2013).

"The Case of the Missing Bicycle." *Texas Gardener Magazine* (2015).

"A Questionable Death." (Agatha-nominated) *History and Mystery, Oh My!* (Mystery and Horror, LLC, 2015).

"The Management of Secrets." *Deadly Nightshade: Best New England Crime Stories* (Crime Spell Books, 2022).

Edith Maxwell Bibliography

Cece Barton Mysteries (Maddie Day)

Christmas Mittens Murder (anthology)	2023
Murder, Uncorked	2023

Country Store Mysteries (Maddie Day)

Flipped for Murder	2015
Grilled for Murder	2016
When the Grits Hit the Fan	2017
Biscuits and Slashed Browns	2018
Death Over Easy	2018
Strangled Eggs and Ham	2019
Christmas Cocoa and a Corpse (anthology)	2019
Nacho Average Murder	2020
Candy Slain Murder	2020
No Grater Crime	2021
Batter Off Dead	2022
Christmas Scarf Murder (anthology)	2022
Four Leaf Cleaver	2023

Cozy Capers Book Group Mysteries (Maddie Day)

Murder on Cape Cod	2018
Murder at the Taffy Shop	2021
Murder at the Lobstah Shack	2021
Murder in a Cape Cottage	2022
Murder at a Cape Bookstore	2023

Quaker Midwife Mysteries (Edith Maxwell)

Delivering the Truth	2016
Called to Justice	2017
Turning the Tide	2018
Charity's Burden	2019
Judge Thee Not	2019
Taken Too Soon	2020
A Changing Light	2021

Local Foods Mysteries (Edith Maxwell)

A Tine to Live, a Tine to Die	2013
'Til Dirt Do Us Part	2014
Farmed and Dangerous	2015
Murder Most Fowl	2016
Mulch Ado About Murder	2017

Lauren Rousseau Mysteries (Edith Maxwell)

Speaking of Murder	2012
Bluffing is Murder on the Bluffs	2014

A Questionable Death

A Questionable Death is printed on 60-pound paper, and is designed by Jeffrey Marks using InDesign. The type is Garamond, named for the 16th century French engraver, Claude Garamon. The cover is by Gail Cross. The first edition was published in two forms: trade softcover, perfect bound; and one hundred copies sewn in cloth, numbered and signed by the author. Each of the clothbound copies includes a separate pamphlet, "Labor's Peril," a short story by Edith Maxwell. *A Questionable Death* was printed by Southern Ohio Printers and bound by Cincinnati Bindery. The book was published in April 2023 by Crippen & Landru Publishers, Inc., Cincinnati, OH.

Crippen & Landru, Publishers
P. O. Box 532057
Cincinnati, OH 45253
Web: www.Crippenlandru.com
E-mail: Orders@crippenlandru.com

Since 1994, Crippen & Landru has published more than 100 first editions of short-story collections by important detective and mystery writers.

This is the best edited, most attractively packaged line of mystery books introduced in this decade. The books are equally valuable to collectors and readers. [Mystery Scene Magazine]

The specialty publisher with the most star-studded list is Crippen & Landru, which has produced short story collections by some of the biggest names in contemporary crime fiction. [Ellery Queen's Mystery Magazine]

God bless Crippen & Landru. [The Strand Magazine]

A monument in the making is appearing year by year from Crippen & Landru, a small press devoted exclusively to publishing the criminous short story. [Alfred Hitchcock's Mystery Magazine]

Crippen & Landru Publications

Challenge the Impossible: The Impossible Files of Dr. Sam Hawthorne by Edward D. Hoch. Full cloth in dust jacket, signed and numbered by the publisher, $45.00. Trade softcover, $19.00.

Nothing Is Impossible: Further Problems of Dr. Sam Hawthorne by Edward D. Hoch.
Dr. Sam Hawthorne, a New England country doctor in the first half of the twentieth century, was constantly faced by murders in locked rooms and impossible disappearances. *Nothing Is Impossible* contains fifteen of Dr. Sam's most extraordinary cases. Full cloth in dust jacket, signed and numbered by the publisher, $45.00. Trade softcover, $19.00.

Chain of Witnesses; The Cases of Miss Phipps by Phyllis Bentley, edited by Marvin Lachman. Lost Classics Series. A critic writes, "stylistically, [Bentley's] stories ... share a quiet humor and misleading simplicity of statement with the works of Christie .... Her work [is] informed and consistent with the classic traditions of the mystery." Full cloth in dust jacket, $29.00. Trade softcover, $19.00.

Swords, Sandals And Sirens by Marilyn Todd.
Murder, conmen, elephants. Who knew ancient times could be such fun? Many of the stories feature Claudia Seferius, the super-bitch heroine of Marilyn Todd's critically acclaimed mystery series set in ancient rome. Others feature Cleopatra, the olympian gods, and high priestess Ilion blackmailed to work with Sparta's feared secret police. Full cloth in dust jacket, signed and numbered by the author, $45.00. Trade softcover, $19.00.

The Puzzles of Peter Duluth by Patrick Quentin. Lost Classics Series.
Anthony Boucher wrote: "Quentin is particularly noted for the enviable polish and grace which make him one of the leading American fabricants of the murderous comedy of manners; but this surface smoothness conceals intricate and meticulous plot construction as faultless as that of Agatha Christie." Full cloth in dust jacket, $29.00. Trade softcover, $19.00.

Hunt in the Dark by Q. Patrick, Lost Classics Series. Full cloth in dust jacket, $29.00. Trade softcover, $19.00.

All But Impossible: The Impossible Files of Dr. Sam Hawthorne by Edward D. Hoch. Full cloth in dust jacket, signed and numbered by the publisher, $45.00. Trade softcover, $19.00.

Sequel to Murder by Anthony Gilbert, edited by John Cooper. Full cloth in dust jacket, $29.00. Trade softcover, $19.00.

Hildegarde Withers: Final Riddles? by Stuart Palmer with an introduction by Steven Saylor. Full cloth in dust jacket, $29.00. Trade softcover, $19.00

Shooting Script by William Link and Richard Levinson, edited by Joseph Goodrich. Full cloth in dust jacket, signed and numbered by the families, $47.00. Trade softcover, $22.00.

Subscriptions

Subscribers agree to purchase each forthcoming publication, either the Regular Series or the Lost Classics or (preferably) both. Collectors can thereby guarantee receiving limited editions, and readers won't miss any favorite stories.

Subscribers receive a discount of 20% off the list price (and the same discount on our backlist) and a specially commissioned short story by a major writer in a deluxe edition as a gift at the end of the year.

The point for us is that, since customers don't pick and choose which books they want, we have a guaranteed sale even before the book is published, and that allows us to be more imaginative in choosing short story collections to issue.

That's worth the 20% discount for us. Sign up now and start saving. Email us at orders@crippenlandru.com or visit our website at www.crippenlandru.com on our subscription page.